PREBEN ANDERSEN

A YEAR IN THE LIFE

OF A VIKING PRINCESS

A BIT OF A FANTASY (BUT WITH A SERIOUS MESSAGE)

FOR CHILDREN AND ADULTS ALIKE

WITH SUPPLEMENT 1 ILLUSTRATIONS BY ESME HARVEY, 9 YEARS OF AGE

* BASED ON JOURNAL NOTES WHICH HAVE ONLY RECENTLY BEEN DISCOVERED *
* COLLATED AND VERIFIED BY THE REVEREND PREBEN ANDERSEN *

I dedicate this book (in descending order age wise) to the following family members: Farah, Maxine, Jay, Cian, Esme, Oscar, Annelise, Isabella, Zach and Anthony. Some are adults, some teenagers, some younger still, and one a toddler. I am grateful to "BRITA" (her Viking name of course) who is truly proud of 'being a Viking like Granddad', and whose imagined journal notes form the basis of this book. In fact, while I have taken many liberties with the chronology of this work, "BRITA" to this day does write her own little journal, which she assures her Mum and Dad "makes me go to sleep better at night." And how lovely is that.

While I have written the book very much for children and with children in mind, I hope and pray that there is also much in it that will appeal to *anyone,* regardless of age, who feel young at heart. And don't we all? I am therefore unable and reluctant to put a precise age range to this book, as really, I write it for everyone. None of the principal characters are given an absolutely specific age, nor are they described in any detail with respect to how they look – much is left to the reader's imagination. MUM and DAD are 'types' rather than a particular couple, and they should not be seen literally as parents to all the children mentioned.

I am grateful to the world wide web in general, and to Google in particular, for providing me so freely and lovingly with historical and interesting facts about Viking life, and also with the royalty free picture for the front of the book, showing The Princess and the Hammershus fortress (see also below). Also thank you for the two royalty free pictures which start the picture gallery in Supplement 1. Most of what you are about to read is pure imagination on my part, and I make no apologies for that. It's been a real joy letting my old brain cells run riot all over the place with this book.

For the most part Vikings originated in Denmark, Norway and Sweden, and so, I have decided to locate much of my story on the small island of Bornholm, which *is* Danish territory, yet situated to the south of Sweden. Bornholm boasts Hammershus, believed to be the oldest medieval fortress in Northern Europe, erected in the 13th century. I have therefore taken a chronological liberty here, as the original Vikings had long since been and gone by the time Hammershus was built! However, for the purposes of my story, Hammershus is the ideal setting for much of the action taking place in BRITA's journal, and it is the location for many of the adventures she and her cousins and nephews are now about to share with us.

Finally, my grateful thanks go to my daughter HEIDI for helping me choose the Viking names from a very long list, and of course to BRITA (aka ESME) for providing the wonderful illustrations in Supplement 1. Some I found on the internet and asked her to copy in her own style, and so, they are all her own design and choice and entirely her own work. Thank you also to TRICIA for proofreading the script for me.

Enjoy the ride!   Preben

I would suggest you take a copy of this page and keep it close to hand for easy reference, at least until you become familiar with all the names. In the book, all the main characters are shown in capitals every time they appear, so that they can be easily identified from the list below. We begin with the Guardians (who are adults) and continue with the eight grandchildren, starting with the oldest, who are both teenagers. In each case, only their Viking names and their meanings are given. I do not mention their real names in this list but do wonder if not some of them may recognize themselves, as we go along? Assuming they read the book or have it read to them of course. Here's praying!

THE PRINCIPAL CHARACTERS

YULLA - Gem of the Sea

INGRID - Beautiful Woman

AIFE – Great Warrior Woman

RUNE - Mystery

BRITA - Little Princess (and the author of this book)

FRIDA - Woman of Peace

LEIF - Descendant, Beloved

LOVA - Battle Noise

BJORN - Bear

SKOLL – Cheers (the very youngest, and please note, he does not appear until the August entries)

THE SUPPORTING CAST

MUM

DAD

OARSMEN

SHIPYARD WORKERS

FARMERS

PRIESTS

AND NEVER FORGETTING "SOMEONE" CALLED ERLING

THE YEAR OF OUR LORD 1000

Monday, January 1st

This year is a leap year, so there will be 29 days in February instead of 28. I am so glad my birthday is not on February 29th, as I would only have a birthday every four years! But good morning, journal, this is BRITA writing, and I plan to do so at least a couple of days every week throughout the year. If I am not too busy, of course, for there is a lot going on here on our little island in the middle of nowhere. Bornholm! I ask you. Did you ever hear of that place until now? Well, this is where I was born, and where I still live with MUM and DAD and my many nieces and nephews, and we all just love it here. MUM and DAD often call me their Little Princess, which of course is what my Viking name means. It is rather sweet.

At first sight, Bornholm is not much more than a big piece of rock in the sea south of Sweden, but when you look closely, there is much more to it than that. We have a large shipyard here, where DAD works, and MUM makes the coffee and prepares the food for the workers. And, of course, we have Hammershus! The House of the Hammer. A great fortress with a lot of history. Most people on the island think that this is where our gods Odin and Thor hung out in the good old days, and where in fact Thor's very own hammer lies hidden somewhere. No one has ever found it, but everyone on the island talks about it.

Thursday, January 4th

Doesn't time fly when you enjoy yourself? But here we are again, and writing on a Thursday, which of course is named after Thor, Thor's day. Odin and Thor were always together, you just could not have one without the other. A lot of our Viking history has to do with Odin and Thor, although I have to say that as DAD and his men keep building longboats and travel the world, it seems that they keep finding other gods out there that we never knew anything about. Sometimes DAD even returns from one of his trips and talks about someone called Jesus, who lived and died about one thousand years ago, but that is adult talk, and I am only a child. You cannot help but listen in, though, always hoping to learn something new.

Anyway, much of my day is taken up with playing with my many nieces and nephews. We have plenty to keep us occupied. Of course, we need to work as well and keep up with reading and writing, but MUM helps with that when she is not busy looking after everybody at the shipyard. Many of our families are farmers or craftsmen who just love working with animals and making things out of wood and steel, and many of our toys are made by our own people. I enjoy the spinning top a lot and the little wooden boats and swords, which the people at the shipyard make with the leftovers from the longboat. We children also love running, jumping and skipping, but most of all we like exploring. YULLA and INGRID are our guardian angels, who always try and keep us in place. They are much older than the seven of us, and in fact AIFE and RUNE are quite old too, they are teenagers after all, so they sometimes think they are in charge. But they are not – the five of us young ones are! Always.

Of course, none of us are old enough to join the men on their voyages, which can often take months and sometimes see them reach the other side of the world, but we can go and explore just where we are. And plan our next adventures.

Wednesday, January 10th

Today, the seven of us (not YULLA and INGRID) finished a week of meetings and planning and talking and drawing, which is why I have not had time to write so much in my journal. It is not always easy to find the time and the place, as the adults get suspicious, if we are away too long, or do not share with them what we are up to. If only they knew!

However, we have had a really good look at the plans and charts we have for Hammershus, and it is interesting to see that there are such a lot of different rooms and buildings in that place, and we think that Thor's hammer may just be hidden in one of them. And if it is, we will find it for sure. We have made a list of the many different parts of Hammershus, and here they are, all empty now of course and probably many of them in a right state, but never mind:

1. The central fortress and the Mantel Tower
2. The Castle Bridge
3. The Brewery and the Bakery
4. The Courthouse
5. The Butter Basement
6. The Dog Tower
7. The Fox Tower
8. The Plum Tower
9. The Storage Rooms

We decided to go away for a few days to decide for ourselves where to start our search for Thor's hammer and then meet again on Monday, with a firm plan of action. Oh, it really is exciting! AIFE and RUNE insisted on being with us again at that meeting, but they agreed that apart from advising YULLA and INGRID that we are up to something, we should be allowed just to get on with it. Knowing that the four 'oldies' are always there for us, if we were to get into any trouble.

Monday, January 15th

BJORN is the youngest in our group. In fact, he has not long been toddling about, which of course is better than crawling. He may well grow into a proper BEAR one day, but for the moment we just call him CUDDLY BEAR for he is, and we love him to bits. But we are a little concerned that once we start invading the fortress for real, he might struggle or get in the way. We wait and see.

We all returned to the planning meeting with our own ideas about where and how to begin, but in the end – and being the journal writer – I, BRITA, had my way, and we are going to start our search for Thor's hammer in THE STORAGE ROOMS. I am sure you will agree that seems an obvious place to begin. FRIDA and LEIF reminded us that perhaps we ought to wait a bit and see off DAD and his men on their new longboat first, which is now almost finished.

We believe our search will be easier with so many of the adults out of the way. LOVA had no objection. Like BJORN she is quite young and tends to go with the flow. Her name might mean Battle Noise, and I am sure one day she will fire on all cylinders. However, for now she seems quite happy, with BJORN, to let the three of us, FRIDA, LEIF and me, BRITA, get on with it. Always carefully supervised, of course, by AIFE and RUNE, the teenagers.

We agreed to meet at the shipyard on Thursday, which is when our newest longboat will launch and head for new horizons. Always a special occasion, with lots of good food to eat and a real party atmosphere.

Friday, January 19th

What a day that was! "Golden Explorer" was launched with DAD as her Captain and 20 oarsmen to do all the hard work. She is just 25 metres long, so I reckon it could be a little bit cramped onboard and that perhaps some of the oarsmen may whack each other round the heads with their oars from time to time, if they don't get the oars synchronised? But they all set sail happily, with lots of food onboard prepared by MUM. I asked DAD where they were off to this time, and he said he didn't really know, but wherever the wind and the oarsmen took them, he guessed. I also asked him how long he might be before returning home, and again he was not sure. "Depends on how often I lose my way", he said, good old DAD. At least he is honest!

I doubt if they will be back for several months, though, so that gives FRIDA and LEIF and me, and of course LOVA and BJORN (bless them, they are only little!) plenty of time to get our thinking caps on and go and explore Hammershus. We cannot wait.

Our guardian angels, YULLA and INGRID, the young and not so young adults, did say before we all left the shipyard that they did not want to hear of any trouble from us, and that we had to listen to and obey AIFE and RUNE all the time. Yes, of course, I said, knowing very well that whenever we can, we shall meet and plan and explore in secret, without AIFE and RUNE being told about it.

And so, the five of us have agreed to meet at the Hammershus ruin on Sunday morning, while the big ones and the adults gather for worship at the service taken by the old PRIEST, whom DAD came across and took captive and brought back with him on one of his voyages, and who has now become part of the family. Not that he speaks much about Odin and Thor, if at all. It seems to be all about Jesus on a Sunday...

Monday, January 22nd

And there was me thinking THE STORAGE ROOMS would be the obvious place to start. Well, no one can get everything right all the time, can they, not even BRITA, the Little Princess, who is writing all this.

For a start, it took the five of us long enough to get there in the first place, as we kept losing track of LOVA and BJORN. No one has ever managed to keep LOVA in line, she is so "get up and go" with everything, afraid of nothing. You really need to have an eye in the back of your head to know what she is up to. And as for BJORN, toddling about in his own little world, his cries of 'Wait for me! Wait for me!" did hold us up for a while. Still, FRIDA, the peaceful one, who always goes about things quietly and persistently, and LEIF, the determined one, who never misses a thing, kept up well with me, and before we knew it, we had arrived at the entrance to the fortress of Hammershus.

It took us a little while to find THE STORAGE ROOMS, despite the detailed maps that AIFE and RUNE, the teenagers, have helped draw up for us, as they are both so artistic. "Be careful," they had told the five of us before we set out, "old ruins may be exciting places to explore, BUT they can be dangerous places too, and we want you all back in one piece and in time for lunch."

In the old days, THE STORAGE ROOMS were used not only for food supplies, but also to store things like corn and timber, which those who could not afford to pay taxes often gave to the keepers of the castle, instead of money. And as we walked round in the rubble, we could still see some traces of corn and timber, despite Hammershus having stood empty for hundreds of years. But all in all, there was not much to see, and most of what we did see we could not tell what was in the first place, so it was rather disappointing.

"Let's find our way back," said FRIDA, "this is getting us nowhere, and there is no sign of a hammer anywhere." "Yes," LEIF agreed, "let's go home. It's only day one of our adventure and there are so many more places to explore. And my stomach is rumbling."

"OK," I said, "perhaps you are right. And the PRIEST must have finished his sermon now and maybe getting near to the end of the service? We don't want to get caught out by MUM or AIFE or RUNE, do we, not to mention YULLA and INGRID."

And so, we returned home, having lost BJORN a couple of times first – "Wait for me! Wait for me!" – and having a job keeping LOVA under control as well. But we got there just as lunch was put on the table, and none of the older ones asked any questions or wondered what we had been up to. Not that there would have been much to tell anyway. I do hope our next trip will be a lot more exciting.

Tuesday, January 23rd

I have to say that after Sunday's disappointing outing to Hammershus, I was not expecting to write so soon again, but this morning YULLA and INGRID came up to me and asked me to join them for a little chat, while FRIDA and LEIF kindly agreed to stay behind and look after the little ones, BJORN and LOVA, who were playing happily with their spinning tops in the yard.

YULLA, being the older and perhaps wiser of the two young adults, began by saying to me, "BRITA, we know you are keen on finding Thor's hammer, and we don't blame you for that, but never forget that if it really is hidden in Hammershus, it will have been there for hundreds of years, and you cannot just expect it to turn up at first sight." And INGRID nodded in agreement and added, "That's right, and chances are of course that it will never be found, no matter where you look."

I must admit that I was not amused to hear this from the two ladies, so I asked them straight out, "So what do you suggest we do now then? Just go and forget all about it?"

"Not at all," said YULLA, "just be patient, and if we were you, don't be afraid to seek advice from AIFE and RUNE as well. After all, they did help you a lot with the drawings. Don't leave them out completely, this is our advice." "Yes," INGRID agreed, "they will not interfere, and they will never do anything you do not ask them to help with, but they will be glad to feel included. Just think about it."

And I did think about it, for all of five seconds anyway, after the young adults had gone and before returning to my four partners. But by the time I got back, I had decided that the five of us should at least have one more go ourselves, before involving anyone else. So, we decided to meet the next day in our secret place, to decide what part of the fortress we should tackle next, and when.

Thursday, January 25th

Yesterday is a day that none of us will ever forget. And what a difference from Sunday, although once again we saw no sign of Thor's hammer. We did see some interesting things, though, that I need to write down, while I remember them.

First of all, at yesterday's meeting we agreed that THE BREWERY AND THE BAKERY looked and sounded interesting. After having carefully located them on AIFE and RUNE'S sketches, we set out quite early in the morning, having of course shared with YULLA and INGRID and MUM what we had decided. MUM prepared lots of good food and drink to take away with us, as she reckoned it could be a long day, and indeed, so it was. AIFE and RUNE saw us off and wished us well, reminding us that if ever we needed their help, just to stop and send a quick smoke signal to them or blow our whistles, and they would come and find us. We said thank you and set off.

Even BJORN seemed to have a new spring in his step this time and did not get lost or slow us down on the way there at all. And LOVA too was well behaved and kept to the beaten track with the rest of us, instead of doing her own thing and going her own way.

We had no trouble finding the right place at all. Although the fortress has stood empty for hundreds of years and is now little more than a pile of broken rock, it was as if certain smells still lingered even after all that time. FRIDA and LEIF noticed it first. "It smells just like when Mum bakes her bread in the kitchen, lovely, but maybe just a bit dusty too? MUM's kitchen never smells dusty" said FRIDA, sharply followed by LEIF, "Phew! It really does smell like a brewery in here. Reminds me of DAD when he gulps down his beer in the pub!" I could but agree, but I had nothing to add, and in any case, something else had caught my attention.

On the stone wall behind the remains of a big stove there was like a sculpture cut into the rock, seemingly with some very sharp instruments, and perhaps a hammer and chisel? It did not look as if it had been completed, maybe something had disturbed the artist, but there was enough there to detect a group of men in white clothing, reclining at a very large table, eating and drinking together. And one of the men seemed to have a big, white shining light all around his head, while the other men were facing him and could not take their eyes off him. I stood in front of the sculpture, spellbound, for a very long time, forgetting all about the lingering smell of bread and beer.

Up until now, the only characters I had ever seen depicted anywhere were Odin and Thor and some of their followers, but this was something else. Even BJORN and LOVA, so young and innocent, could tell that this was a different kind of moment and stood still beside me for several minutes, before quietly wandering off again. I decided there and then to speak to the PRIEST when we got back, thinking that he might have an explanation.

Before that, and when we had finished exploring the rest of the BREWERY AND THE BAKERY, without finding anything of interest, we decided to have one more peep inside THE STORAGE ROOMS. Just in case we had missed something important on Sunday. I wish now we hadn't, for BJORN AND LOVA got seriously lost, and it took the rest of us the best part of an hour to find them again, with the help of our whistles. The embarrassing part was that when we blew our whistles, AIFE and RUNE thought we were calling them, and they both came running, with their helmets on, prepared for battle, both being very sporty and well trained in physical exercise. I had to tell them that we were not in any danger, but BJORN and LOVA had gone missing, although we had caught up with them again now. Oh dear…

When we finally got home, MUM stood waiting for us together with YULLA and INGRID, and I must admit that none of them looked too pleased. "Where on earth have you been?", said MUM, "it's well gone your bedtimes, well, for most of you anyway, and I'm in a good mind to put you all under house arrest for a day or two. You can be grateful that DAD isn't here, or he would have something to say! Now, off you go, get ready for bed, no supper for any of you tonight!"

Of course, AIFE and RUNE did get their supper, as after all they had come to save us. And YULLA and INGRID had already eaten together with MUM, so they were alright. But as for the rest of us, did we feel embarrassed!

Just before going to sleep, I promised myself to try and get hold of the PRIEST, sooner rather than later, as that sculpture on the wall in the BREWERY AND THE BAKERY kept playing on my mind. Tomorrow, maybe?

Sunday, January 28th

Well, Friday came and went. We all thought that after Thursday's home-coming, we ought to lie low the next day, so we just tried to do everything to please MUM and YULLA and INGRID. We concentrated on our reading and writing and played quietly with our toys in between as well. It seemed to work okay.

AIFE and RUNE walked round with big grins on their faces, as if to say, "Serves them right!" but for most of the day they left us well alone.

The five of us decided NOT to meet to plan anything for our next adventure, but to let the dust settle first. However, just before supper, I did manage to sneak out and find the old PRIEST in his house. He could not see me right that minute but said to me that I could come back tomorrow morning when he would gladly give me an hour of his time. And so, we arranged to meet at 10 o'clock on the Saturday. He did not know what I wanted him for, and I did not say anything.

It was not easy to get away from the others without giving anything away on the Saturday morning. In the end I just said I had an important meeting with someone, but that I would share with everyone what happened as soon as I got back. I put FRIDA and LEIF in charge of the two little ones, LOVA and BJORN, and they seemed happy with that. And off I went for my meeting with the PRIEST.

Before I could even say why I had come, he started by asking me a question. "BRITA," he said, "can you remember when I first arrived here as a prisoner on one of DAD's longboats? And have you ever wondered why he decided to capture only me and bring **me** back here, and no one else?"

I had to admit that no, I couldn't remember when I first saw the PRIEST among us, and no, I didn't even know what country he had come from. But I also said to him that he was now so much part of our little community, just like one of us, and we loved having him around. A little flattery can go a long way!

He seemed touched by that and continued, "DAD found me when he and his men landed in Egypt, on the river Nile, five years ago. DAD told me that not for the first time had they lost their way completely, and the only reason they grabbed hold of me that day was that I had gone to the river to fetch water for the people in the village I served. I was not married, I had no family, and I was the only one around by the river. So, DAD and one of his oarsmen took hold of me and whisked me onboard, before they set sail for home. But they were kind enough to me and treated me well on the long journey home, perhaps because I was a PRIEST? And on the way home, I had plenty of time to share with DAD and his 20 oarsmen about Jesus."

Here the PRIEST paused his long narrative and seemed miles away in his own thoughts. I coughed gently, and when I saw that he was back with me, I said, "Who is this Jesus? I have only ever known about Odin and Thor and gods like that, but I do know that you often speak about Jesus on a Sunday." The PRIEST laughed at that, took my hand, and said, "Not only on a Sunday, BRITA, but every moment of every day and to everyone I meet."

"What does this Jesus look like," I asked. "I mean, we know that Odin wears a great big helmet and has a wild long beard and a fierce glimpse in his eyes, and that Thor is almost as tough and has the use of a mighty hammer. We also know that when there is thunder and lightning that is when Odin and Thor are angry with us, and it is their way of letting us know."

The PRIEST smiled and said, "Well, I rather think that when we hear the thunder that is when our Father God and His Son Jesus move furniture around in Heaven, to make more room for people like us, when our time has come to go and meet with them."

I was not quite sure what to say to that, but in my heart, I realized that since the PRIEST had arrived there had been almost as much talk about Jesus on the island of Bornholm than old rumours and memories about Odin and Thor. It was as if something new was taking over from the old…

After a long pause, I finally summoned up the courage to say to the PRIEST, "FRIDA and LEIF and LOVA and BJORN and I went to the castle the other day, to the KITCHEN AND THE BREWERY. And we found a kind of sculpture that looked unfinished, with a group of men reclining at a big table, having a meal, and with one man, all in white, surrounded by a big, shining light round his head. Can you tell me what that was all about?"

Again, the PRIEST took me gently by the hand and said, "BRITA, why don't you and your four nieces and nephews come and join the rest of us at church one Sunday? I have to say that I don't even need one finger to count how many times I have seen any of you for service. If only you come, you will get to know a lot more about Jesus, week by week, I promise you."

Soon after that I left the PRIEST, deep in thought. I knew I would not be going to church in the morning, as I would be far too busy writing in my Journal, and indeed I am, as you can see. When I got back from my meeting, and after lunch, my four partners wanted to know what I had been up to without them. I put them off by saying that there was far too much for me to share with them right now, and I needed to get things clear first in my own head. They then asked when we should meet again to plan our next adventure, but I was not able to fix a day or a time there and then. The PRIEST had given me much to think about, and I needed space.

They were not happy, but they did leave me alone for the rest of the day.

Tuesday, January 30ᵗʰ

We had arranged to meet yesterday to decide which of the four big – and not so big – Towers to tackle next, but our plans were well and truly scuppered, when on the distant horizon we saw the 'Golden Explorer' returning home. And when a couple of hours later DAD blew his Viking Horn, as a signal for MUM to start laying the table for all her hungry men.

MUM could not understand for a moment how they could be back this soon, barely ten full days since they left. She could only assume that DAD had once again lost his way terribly, and his men had begged him to return home, as otherwise where on earth might they end up?

However, over lunch all became clear when DAD explained – after having downed his fifth pint of beer in half an hour - that their voyage this time had only taken them to the southern part of Norway. Where after a pleasant and relaxing time south-east in calm waters up through a big fiord, they had reached a large settlement, which the people there announced would be their capital city, and which they intended to name Christiania. "That's a funny name," DAD had said when he heard this, "why not call it Thor's Bay or Odin's Town or something to please our gods?" To which one of the locals replied, "Well, we have to call it something, don't we?" DAD had nodded, none the wiser. He just could not see any rhyme or reason for naming a city Christiania. And who is he anyway when he's at home, DAD thought. Or is it named after a she?

The locals had not been in the least bit scared by the Danish Viking invasion. After all, most of them were Norwegian Vikings themselves. Even after DAD and his twenty men had donned their helmets to look scary, many of the Norwegians only laughed and carried on with what they were doing, which was building their city. DAD and his men decided to stay on 'Golden Explorer' for a couple of days – after all, they still had plenty of MUM'S food and drink left – and so they departed on their return journey, having made no real friends, but no enemies either. "Yes, it was a bit of a weird journey," said DAD, "perhaps the next one will be more exciting? Anyway, what has been going on here, while we've been away?"

He looked at me when he asked the question, as if I were the one with all the answers. But I glanced firmly at my nieces and nephews, so none of us said anything apart from "Oh, you know, the usual, playing and reading and writing, and doing what we are told." Through the corner of my eye, I saw YULLA and INGRID shake their heads, but they said nothing. And RUNE punched AIFE in the ribs, when he was about to disagree, so we all had a lucky escape. MUM too kept her thoughts to herself. It was only when the PRIEST stood up and spoke that I wished there was a nearby hole I could bury myself in.

"BRITA came to see me on Saturday," he started, "and we had a really good talk together, she and I." DAD looked puzzled at first but then pleased, and, in any case, he was too busy eating and drinking together with his twenty oarsmen to say a lot.

"Yes," the PRIEST continued. "A really good talk we had, BRITA and I, so we did." As no one commented, the PRIEST decided to change to another subject.

"Christiania," he said, "and Norway. I find it interesting that this is where you should get to. Quite close and easy to return to when they have finished building their city. I wouldn't mind joining you next time if I may?"

"Yes," Dad thought to himself, but without saying it out loud. "And perhaps you will like it so much that you stay there? Perhaps you may even find your Jesus there?" But he said none of this out loud, he only told me later that these were his thoughts. Knowing, of course, that no one can hear or see what you think.

"Maybe," DAD said instead to the PRIEST, "but it won't be for a while yet. By Odin and Thor, we are tired, early bed for us today."

Before the twenty-one men retired to their rooms, DAD cast one last look at me and said, "I will speak to you again in a day or two, BRITA. I feel there is something you are not telling me."

Thursday, February 1st

FRIDA, LEIF, LOVA, BJORN and I decided to spend yesterday doing something which we hoped would please DAD. And, having put our idea past AIFE and RUNE first, we therefore assembled at the shipyard, nice and early, to do a spot of cleaning and tidying up on the 'Golden Explorer'. For, as always, when the men returned from a voyage, the boat was in quite a state, keeping it tidy not being on the top of DAD's priority list.

So, we washed it down, and we cleaned away, and we polished for hours on end, until the boat looked so splendid and shone to the high heavens like never before. It took us all morning, but we were pleased that when we returned home, DAD and his men were still fast asleep and did not know a thing about it. We did not expect a medal for what we had done, but just maybe DAD might forget that he wanted a serious word with his Princess?

INGRID and YULLA, when they heard what we had been up to, walked down to inspect the boat and came back to congratulate us all on a job very well done.

Pleased with ourselves, we felt therefore that we could enjoy lunch and then arrange to meet in our secret place to plan our next expedition. And we did.

Now, Hammershus had four towers when it was first built, namely THE DOG TOWER, THE FOX TOWER, THE PLUM TOWER and THE MANTEL TOWER, which was part of the central fortress, the middle section of the castle. When AIFE and RUNE did their sketches, they were quick to point out that in their opinion, THE MANTEL TOWER looked the most interesting and certainly the tallest of the four. Standing six stories high and with walls up to two metres thick. Imagine, six floors – would BJORN ever manage that? And would we be able to keep LOVA under control? We soon decided that if we were serious about clambering that high, and with all the rubble sure to get in the way, we would all need to wear our helmets and be very careful indeed.

AIFE and RUNE told us that when the tower was first built, it contained all the weapons and cannons and cannon balls that were needed to defend not just the castle itself but the whole island of Bornholm as well. And they also told us that for many years the tower was used as a prison. All very exciting, but what were the chances, I asked myself, of finding Thor's hammer there?

But then I thought, Hammershus has so many different sides to it and already seems full of surprises, so let's go and explore.

We decided to meet, properly equipped and with helmets on our heads, on Saturday. Perhaps there were a few other things we could do first tomorrow to keep MUM and DAD happy?

Sunday, February 4th

As it happened, we did not need to worry about behaving ourselves on Friday as neither MUM and DAD nor any of the oarsmen were around much. As often happened, when there were no plans to sail anywhere, the seafarers would wander off and help the neighbouring farmers, who always could do with volunteers. They never got paid anything for helping, BUT they were treated to some lovely meals on the farms by way of a thank you.

There is this misunderstanding in many places that Vikings are always on the warpath, always up for a fight, always out and about looking for new places to conquer, but that is not true. Most of the time we are just ordinary people, minding our own business, working hard, and getting on with life like everybody else.

I am writing this after church and before lunch. YES, I went to church this morning after MUM and DAD had set off early to help on the farms. I had intended to go on my own, but RUNE and AIFE came along too, as they always did on a Sunday, and sat each side of me as THE PRIEST took to the lectern. All the others stayed at home, and most were probably asleep after yesterday's adventures at THE MANTEL TOWER. And who can blame them? It was a day and a half!

I must confess I am not sure how much I got out of the sermon this morning. I only came to when RUNE shook me and said, "Come on! Time to go home." But at least I went, and THE PRIEST seemed pleased to see me, when I shook his hand on the way out.

Anyway, I don't think I have ever seen a tower as tall as THE MANTEL TOWER, and the narrow and winding route up to the top was dangerous and slippery. We were all grateful for our hats. BJORN (as you would expect) slipped a couple of times on the way up, and more times than I could count on the way down. And LOVA wasn't far behind him either. But FRIDA, LEIF and I managed between us to keep them under control with strict warnings to behave themselves.

From the top of the tower there was the most wonderful view of the whole island. We could clearly see 'Golden Explorer' in her shipyard, the settlement where we all lived, the church and the house where the PRIEST hung out. And, of course, the many farm buildings with herds of cows, sheep, and horses, where we knew MUM and DAD and their twenty men would be working hard for most of the day.

It was a bright day. Snow and ice had not yet come to Bornholm, and as children we often heard the adults say how strange that was, at a time of year, February, where often it was impossible to get anywhere except by ski or sledge, as everything was frozen over. Not so this year. The adults praised Odin and Thor for looking after us all so well with the weather, so we could continue to work. Except THE PRIEST, who praised God and Jesus. It takes all sorts.

Anyway, did we find Thor's hammer in the tower? No, we did not. Did we find anything else of interest instead? Not really. Except, when I think about it, where the prisoners used to be locked up, there were still bits of chain and what looked like hand and foot cuffs on the ground. We threatened BJORN and LOVA that if they forgot to behave, we would tie them up and hang them from the wall without food or drink, until we came and freed them again, whenever that might be. "Oh, BRITA, you are naughty," LEIF said to me, "it's a good thing we know you don't mean it." "Who says I don't?", I said.

It was on the long cumbersome way down, holding on to the wall for dear life, when FRIDA suddenly stopped in her tracks, with her hand stuck in a hole in the wall. Well, she was able to move the hand just a bit, enough to loosen a few stones and make the hole bigger. It was then that we realized we were looking through that hole into a small hidden chamber, which we had not noticed on the way up.

We took it in turns to peep through the hole to decide whether there was anything there worth exploring, and if so, how to go about it, as we did not carry any tools to dig our way in there today. We could not immediately see anything, until LOVA of all people shouted out loud, "Look, BRITA, there is something in there, something bright and quite shiny, but I cannot see what it is." I had not been able to think and dream of much else since that find in the BREWERY AND THE BAKERY, and although this did not sound like another sculpture, I just about remembered something THE PRIEST had said in his sermon today, before I dozed off. Something about Christianity being new and exciting and full of surprises, and that we have only just started finding out about it on the island of Bornholm. I think that's what he said anyway. He does waffle a bit sometimes. Just like DAD in fact.

We decided to earmark the small chamber in the MANTEL TOWER for a special visit one day. We got home just before MUM and DAD returned from their work on the farms and we arranged to take a few days rest before meeting again in our secret place, to look at the next port of call. And we also agreed that we would leave the small chamber for a while and stick to one of the other sites we had already planned first. "Let's meet on Tuesday afternoon," I said, "and I will ask AIFE and RUNE if they can join us too. If we are going to ask them some time to help us especially with the small chamber, it is just as well if they come to one of our normal meetings first. But we won't go on about the small chamber yet, that is for another day." All agreed.

Wednesday, February 7th

What a good meeting we had yesterday. And not only did AIFE and RUNE join in, but we also had the two 'oldies', YULLA and INGRID, popping their heads in this time. So, we were a full team with all nine of us present. I did make it quite clear that as the Viking Princess and team leader I was the one in charge, and if there was ever anything we had to make a final decision on, I would have the casting vote.

And so, we sat down and looked at all the drawings, and the venue that really caught our attention this time was THE COURTHOUSE. Before we got that far, I did have to stop LOVA from going on about the small chamber, but I just sent her one of my fierce looks, which seemed to do the trick. BJORN seemed quite frightened, so I must have been convincing. AIFE and RUNE just laughed and shook their heads. No respect from those two.

"THE COURTHOUSE, eh?", said YULLA. "Yes, that sounds exciting. Does anyone know anything about it? It's years and years since INGRID and I have been anywhere near the old ruins up there.

AIFE and RUNE, who were after all the masterminds behind the maps and drawings, looked at me for permission to speak. "BRITA," they said as with one voice, "we can tell you a thing or two, if we may." "OK," I said, "but one at a time, please, otherwise it gets confusing." BJORN had already looked away, this was far too much for him, and LOVA did not seem far behind.

"Right then," said AIFE, "Ladies first, if you please." RUNE smiled sweetly at her and stayed quiet. "THE COURTHOUSE," said AIFE, "is in the eastern part of the fortress, and it is basically the basement of what used to be an impressive and large house. This is where they used to have their Court of Law, and where thieves and other criminals were sentenced, before being taken to the gallows on the hills north of the building."

"Oh my," said LEIF and FRIDA, who had been very quiet until now, "How exciting. Does that mean we might find some dead bodies up there?"

"I think not," said RUNE, "they are surely well buried and hidden from view by now, but we might find other things of interest. And don't forget we shall start at THE COURTHOUSE, not on the hills."

"We?", I said, "do you and AIFE intend to come along as well?" "Yes, I wondered about that too" said LOVA, "I did not think we were going to have you two along, until we return to the small chamber…." I stopped her right there with another fierce look, only this time it was too late.

"Small chamber?", said RUNE, "What small chamber? BRITA, what have you been up to that we don't know about?" And YULLA and INGRID also wanted to know and looked at me for answers.

"That's all for another day," I said, "let's just concentrate on THE COURTHOUSE for now. But yes, if RUNE and AIFE want to join us for that, why not? Shall we meet here tomorrow morning at say 10 o'clock and go from there? Are we all happy with that?"

YULLA and INGRID had no objection and seemed quite relieved that they were not also asked to come along. "Just be careful," they said, "but at least you will have RUNE and AIFE to keep an eye. We will tell MUM and DAD where you are planning to go. It is only fair that they know."

I would have preferred to keep MUM and DAD out of it, but in any case, there was little if anything they could do about it, as they were both so busy on the farms. "Tomorrow morning it is then," I said, "and I think best if we wear our helmets again. It may be slippery, and there may be low ceilings in the COURTHOUSE basement. And just to remind you all," I finished, "It is Thor's hammer we are looking for. With all this chatting and coming and going we can sometimes forget."

And so, I closed the meeting with a short prayer to Odin and Thor for safe passage tomorrow for us all. Although deep in my heart something else THE PRIEST had said on Sunday began to stir, but I could not quite put my hand on it…

Friday evening, February 9th

Overnight the first snowfall of the year found its way to Bornholm, and it wasn't just any old snowfall either. The snow lay thick and solid, as we ventured out on our journey. Not only did we all wear our helmets, but, because of the snow, we dragged a couple of big sledges behind us packed with drink and food – yes, kindly prepared by MUM – just in case we got stuck in another snowstorm coming back.

RUNE and AIFE kindly led us, each of them holding LOVA and BJORN firmly by the hand, as they were the youngest. This also meant that the rest of us would just have to stay in line, much to LEIF and FRIDA's disgust, and I wasn't too happy either. We'd rather just get on with it.

So, we skidded, and we slipped, and we tumbled - but managed to get up again well enough – and what would normally have taken us less half an hour to get to the fortress became double that. Exhausted before we even got started, we decided to stop at the house with the basement and have something to eat and drink first, to keep the cold at bay, for it was freezing.

Refreshed with good food and drink, we left the sledges under cover, just outside the ruins of the big house, and found the entrance to the basement. RUNE and AIFE led the way, still holding on to LOVA and BJORN. When we were all safely downstairs, we immediately felt very much warmer than we had earlier, and we were amazed at the size of THE COURTHOUSE and how well preserved it was. Yes, there were bits of it in ruin, as you would expect, but much was in excellent condition, including the very large chair and desk where the chief judge would have sat, and the smaller but still impressive smaller chairs on each side of the middle section. This is where the jury would have sat and dished out their punishment. We really felt as if we had gone back in time.

Imagine my surprise and delight when on the desk of the chief judge I saw a hammer! Yes, a real hammer! Was this it? Had I found Thor's hammer already? Until RUNE got me back to earth with a bump, when he said, "Don't kid yourself, BRITA, this is no more Thor's hammer than I am the king of Pennsylvania! At best, what you see here is the instrument that the judge would have used either to bang the table to keep everyone in order OR use when the sentence was given out. Like, "to the gallows with him" or "five years in prison for her" or – what do I know? But certainly, Thor's hammer it isn't."

AIFE agreed – but then, she would (those two always stuck together) – and I just let it pass and suggested we move on to something else, as the hall was large, and there seemed plenty to look at.

On the walls some of the tapestry was still in quite good condition, and as you would expect from a lawcourt, the motifs were of prisoners and gallows and guillotines and other means of punishment. We could tell that LOVA and BJORN were uncomfortable with it all. LEIF and FRIDA did not look very happy either. On the floor the scraps of carpet, although worn, still showed traces of footsteps, and even signs of some of the prisoners, unable to walk, being dragged across the room to the gate, which led either to the cells or to the hill, where they would end their days. Even I shivered a bit when I realized what kind of a place this was.

"I don't like it here," said BJORN, and the rest of us were quite relieved to hear that, as to be honest we had all had enough. "Let's go back up and get some more to eat and drink before we head for the hills," said FRIDA, and we aimed for the gateway, through which we had entered the basement.

But could we get out? No, we could not, for although we had only been here less than half an hour, another snowstorm had hit Bornholm, and our entrance – which was now our longed-for exit – was blocked with snow. We had nothing except our hands to try and move the white stuff, and AIFE and RUNE did the donkey work, but even they found it hard going. "Will we ever get out?" said BJORN. "Don't be so silly," said LOVA, moments before she got sprayed with big snowflakes coming from AIFE and RUNE's handiwork.

When we finally did get out, the sledges with all the food and drink were covered with snow as well. "Never mind," said LEIF, "at least it has kept cool for us." AIFE and RUNE decided, seeing there were not that many provisions left, to bag them up and carry them over their shoulders, so that BJORN and LOVA could sit on the sledges, pulled by – yes, you guessed it, - FRIDA and me. Talk about distribution of labour. LEIF was the only one, who had only himself to think about, as we struggled our way to the hills. Not to find any traces of dead bodies, but to enjoy a couple of hours of downhill sledding, which made us feel a lot warmer.

We did not get back home until quite late at night, frozen but happy after what could have been a miserable day, but which ended well with a lot of fun.

We spent yesterday very quietly in our own little corners, which is why it is only now I have found the energy to write again. It is almost as if yesterday did not happen at all!

Friday, February 16th

The snow may have come late, but boy, now it's here there is no let up. Everything is covered, the shipyard lies idle, the farm animals are under cover in their stables. MUM and DAD have little to do, the PRIEST sometimes preaches to himself on a Sunday, as most people decide to stay at home. Everything is quiet, uncannily so. And towering over us all is the fortress, the castle, probably breathing a sigh of relief at being left alone for a few days.

The sea surrounding Bornholm is frozen, so no ships can enter or leave the island. Thankfully MUM always ensures there is plenty of bread to make, and milk to get from the farm animals, so we do not go without. We just get so bored.

DAD and his OARSMEN are getting impatient too, they want to set sail again and find new horizons – or do a return trip to Norway to see how they are getting on with Christiania. But that too will have to wait, and of course there is no guarantee that they will ever find Christiania again, knowing DAD's poor sense of direction. Now, what is it about that name, Christiania? It's something the PRIEST said, or didn't say but insinuated, but I can't remember…

Monday, February 19th

I did make it to church yesterday, and THE PRIEST was really pleased to see me make the effort. There were only about six of us there, none of my nephews or nieces went, and YULLA and INGRID gave it a miss too. In fact, I don't think they are very impressed with our last visit to Hammershus, probably thinking that we could have got into real trouble. Had it not been for AIFE and RUNE keeping an eye on us. They avoid us most of the time now.

THE PRIEST was on about forgiveness yesterday. How we must all learn to forgive others, even when they have done, or we think they have done, something really bad. I must admit I can think of loads of examples of BJORN and LOVA being naughty, and how I found it impossible then to forgive them for a very long time, if ever. The PRIEST also said that Jesus – that name again – never holds on to or remembers our sins once we have said sorry and promised never to perform that sin again. I sometimes wonder does that mean we can go and do something else just as naughty? I must ask THE PRIEST next time I see him.

The snow is still coming down hard as I write this. I cannot see any of us meeting for a while. I'm getting bored with it all. There is only so much sledding one can do or snowball fights, and I sense the others are getting tired of it too.

Monday, February 26th

Another week gone, but at least the snow has now almost disappeared and has been replaced with the great thaw. Water everywhere! Which pleases DAD, for now he can at least start thinking about his next voyage. I think he is keen to get back to Christiania, to see how they are getting on there with their new settlement. And this time he wants THE PRIEST to come along too. Why? I am not sure, but the fact is of course that he picked him up on the river Nile in Egypt years ago, so maybe he has had enough of him now and wants to deposit him somewhere else?

I know DAD is not always happy with THE PRIEST, and what he preaches on a Sunday. "By Odin and Thor," DAD said only the other day, "Where is that man coming from? And don't let him put silly ideas into your head, my Princess, they won't do you any good at all." I know DAD does not like me going to listen to THE PRIEST on a Sunday, but I cannot help myself, even if sometimes none of the others can be bothered to join me.

It is almost a month since DAD and 'Golden Explorer' returned from Norway, so no wonder DAD is getting impatient. We always know when he gets bored and frustrated, and we try to keep well out of the way, but yesterday after church I did go and see him, as I had something on my heart.

"DAD," I started, "Is there any chance that I might be able to join you and the oarsmen on your next trip? And is it true that you are thinking of inviting THE PRIEST?" I had been very reluctant to ask, for I knew that his first thought would be, "But what about all my nephews and nieces, if they did not have their Princess to guide and play with them?" But surprisingly, DAD did not say no, in fact he did not say anything at all, only a few hours later I saw him in deep conversation with MUM. I thought no more of it there and then.

Wednesday, February 28th

MUM and DAD called us all together yesterday for a meeting. My first thought was, "Oh, boy, we're in for it now. Either THE PRIEST has grassed on us, or YULLA and INGRID have complained to them about our escapades to the castle. Or AIFE and RUNE have got fed up with being left out of so much of the fun (although we did tag them along for our last trip). The possibilities seemed endless, and I must admit I feared the worst.

DAD stood up when we were all gathered and started liked this: "You won't be surprised to hear that my OARSMEN and I are getting itchy feet, and now that the snow has almost disappeared, we think it is time for our next voyage. And we are planning a return to Christiania, to see how they are getting on there. Any questions so far?"

DAD looked at me especially, but the glance he sent me did not encourage me to say anything, so I didn't.

"Right then," DAD continued. "Golden Explorer is pretty much shipshape or certainly will be in just a few days, so we expect to set sail and dip the oars in early March. And this time we have decided to have some invited guests with us too."

We all sat up and listened intently at this, but still none of us said anything.

"First of all, we are taking THE PRIEST. He goes on and on about Christiania, thinks it is such a beautiful name for a settlement, as it has Christ in it (and who is he when he's at home I ask myself?). But seeing that THE PRIEST is so keen to get there, I have invited him, and perhaps we might just leave him there too?" DAD giggled, but I looked at him a little worried, which he noticed.

"Yes, BRITA, my Little Princess, any problem with that? I know you'd like to go too, but I think you're too young, and after all, FRIDA, LEIF, LOVA and BJORN rely on you to keep them together. I am sure you will have plenty to do anyway, while we're away."

"You haven't mentioned YULLA and INGRID or AIFE and RUNE so far. Does that mean they are invited too?" I couldn't believe I had dared ask DAD the question.

MUM and DAD smiled at this, and MUM now took over where DAD had finished. "Yes, BRITA, we think it is time that the four older ones had a chance to see a bit of the world, but don't worry, I'll stay behind, I'll be here, to keep an eye on the five of you."

My heart sank. How would this affect our planned adventures? How would the five of us be able to continue to explore the castle, with MUM constantly watching us? And we still had so many parts of it to go. This would require some serious planning, and as always it would be up to me, BRITA, to sort it out.

I chose to say nothing, and nobody else did, so the meeting came to an end, and we went our different ways. "Wait for me!", said BJORN, who as always was a bit slow on the uptake.

When I got home, I said to myself, "There is NO WAY that this is going to stop me in my tracks. I'll make sure we get round it somehow. Let "Golden Explorer" be on her way, and then I shall call the shots, as only I can." I could tell my four little friends were disappointed at the outcome of the meeting, although I am not sure how much they understood. Now it would be up to me to make them feel happy again.

Thursday, February 29th

Not that there is much to write since yesterday, but this is a leap year, and it will be another four years before we have another February 29th. That's all I want to say. All those who are going to Christiania are busy getting the ship ready, and MUM, of course, is busy with the provisions they are taking. Enough to feed at least 5,000 people, if you ask me. Now, where on earth did that thought come from? Is it something else I remember THE PRIEST saying?

Monday, March 4th

Well, they're off, and good riddance to them, that's all I can say. The four 'oldies' looked ever so pleased with themselves, as they stood on deck, letting the OARSMEN do all the hard work, and waving goodbye. In fairness, AIFE did shout to us that she would get a courier to send back messages to us, when they stopped on the way, to let us know how they got on. And for us to let them know also how we got on too with exploring the castle. As for RUNE, he just stood there with a mysterious grin on his face, but then that is precisely what his name means, Mystery. YULLA and INGRID we did not see much off. They were already below deck to unpack and store MUM's carefully prepared food and drink. And I just knew that once they had finished, they would be having a close look at the OARSMEN to seek out the most attractive ones for a bit of company later. After all, you cannot row forever, you need to let the sails do their bit too.

DAD? Yes, poor DAD. He was busy trying to make sense of the maps, so that hopefully this time they could find the direct way to Norway, and not end up on the other side of the world instead. At least they have RUNE onboard this time, and when he has finished grinning, perhaps he will give DAD a hand, as he is good with maps.

And so, DAD asked Odin and Thor for a safe crossing, THE PRIEST followed on by asking Jesus for the same (much to DAD's annoyance) and the five of us waved them all off. For what else could we do? MUM shed a little tear before returning home, but not before warning us not to be late for dinner and putting me, BRITA, in charge of the group. No need to say this, Mother, I always am.

Free at last! "Come on," I said to my four remaining friends, "let's find somewhere soon, where we can sit and look through what we have done, and where we have been so far. There is still a lot to do, so get your thinking caps on. We'll meet here at the harbour on Wednesday morning, how about that? 10 o'clock, no later. And do come with ideas!"

Wednesday, March 6th

I am writing this just before bedtime, and I am pleased to say that we had a pretty good meeting this morning. As a matter of fact, for once it was not me who came up with the ideas to start with, but FRIDA. While LEIF, LOVA and BJORN were happy just to be there and let us older ones get on with it.

"I think," FRIDA started, "we should concentrate on some more towers, as there seems to be such a lot of them. I mean, we've done THE MANTEL TOWER, but that still leaves THE DOG TOWER, THE PLUM TOWER and THE FOX TOWER to do. Perhaps we could have a look at AIFE and RUNE's drawings and see what they were used for in the old days. And then decide which one might be interesting to look at more closely?"

"By all means," I said, "are we all in agreement?" LEIF, LOVA and BJORN nodded.

And so, for the next hour I took the lead again and guided us through the sketches prepared by AIFE and RUNE.

It turned out that THE DOG TOWER was used originally both as a watchtower to defend the island from invaders, and as a tower for prisoners. Here those condemned to death would spend their final days overlooking the gallows on the rock below the fortress. Some centuries later, the tower was partly demolished and then rebuilt as a battery for the cannons defending the island.

THE PLUM TOWER is the best-preserved part of Hammershus, although it has been without a roof for centuries. This too was an important part of the island's defence. The keeper of this tower had his own heated and very luxurious rooms, whereas the prisoners, who were taken here, did not enjoy the same comforts. The tower is named after the flowery, coloured and patterned bricks it was made of, with many of them in the colours of ripe plums.

Finally, THE FOX TOWER is one of the more recent additions to the fortress, and again this was used for defence of the island, but not to hold prisoners. Like some other parts of the castle, it was named after animals, as people hoped the alertness and intelligence of many animals, such as foxes, would reflect on those humans, who were responsible for the defence of the castle.

Most of this went well above the heads of LOVA and BJORN, who sat there smiling sweetly as the rest of us tried to make sense of everything.

"So, where do we start, and when?", I said finally. "Let's go and do all three of them in one go," said FRIDA. "The towers do not seem that far apart from each, so I reckon we can do them in one day." LEIF agreed, and LOVA and BJORN just nodded, probably hoping to get it all over with.

We decided to tell MUM what we were up to and then meet again in a couple of days. Just in case any of us changed our minds about things.

Saturday, March 9th

Well, our latest expedition did not come to anything. We woke up to news from a sole courier, who arrived at the harbour in his small dinghy, that AIFE and RUNE would be on their way back home soon, the moment they found some transport to take them. Apparently, they had already had enough of DAD and THE PRIEST arguing and going on and on about this Jesus, and how he was so different from Odin and Thor. Not even a week at sea, and the two would be joining us again soon. I do not know whether to laugh or cry. But thinking about it, without them we would not have found out so much about the three towers. So, I guess it is only fair that we now wait, so that they can accompany us later in the month?

The courier did not mention YULLA or INGRID, so we can only assume that they are still looking for prospective husbands among the OARSMEN? Who knows? Or maybe they will wait until they arrive in Christiania? There might be some handsome "talent" among the Norwegians for them?

The five of us met briefly yesterday and decided to wait for AIFE and RUNE to arrive, hoping that they would not take too long about it. MUM seemed quite relieved. I do not think she is all that pleased about our escapades, without the necessary supervision.

Tuesday, March 12th

AIFE and RUNE are back and boy, did they go on to MUM and the five of us about the arguments between DAD and THE PRIEST. They just could not take it anymore, and fortunately a small vessel, heading for Bornholm anyway, was able to carry them home. Apparently, when they left, the "Golden Explorer" was only a couple of days' journey from Christiania, weather permitting, and AIFE and RUNE bid their farewells with DAD screaming at THE PRIEST that "If he did not shut up soon with all his talk about God and Jesus, he [DAD] would chuck him in the sea and just hope that he could swim the rest of the way to Norway." All heart is DAD.

There is a big welcome back dinner for the two, and of course the rest of us, tonight, so we shall not be able to plan anything regarding the three towers for a little while yet. Ah well, but I must admit I am getting itchy feet. It's over a month now since our last expedition, we really must get going again soon. Perhaps tomorrow all seven of us can get together?

Friday, March 15th

Well, where do I begin? We did meet on Wednesday morning and finally, early yesterday morning, we set off to the three Towers. AIFE and RUNE holding the maps and leading the rest of us, as always trying to make sure that LOVA and BJORN could keep up without getting themselves lost.

But what I really want to share here is the fact that while the lot of them were busy exploring the three towers – without finding anything at all, I should say, of any great interest - I, BRITA, managed to sneak off on my own, back to MANTEL TOWER and that shining thing that FRIDA first noticed, remember? Well, I guessed she had probably forgotten all about it, whereas I hadn't. Nor had I forgotten about that sculpture with the man with the halo surrounded by so many men at table. That had to wait, though, one thing at a time.

So, I sneaked off without the others seeing me, and lo and behold, I managed to find the hidden chamber in the MANTEL TOWER, and I was delighted to see that whatever it was, lying there, shining brightly, had remained untouched and unharmed by all the snow and debris, which no doubt kept falling from time to time. This time, and being on my own, I climbed through the narrow passage and picked up the thing.

It was beautiful. It was golden. It was in the shape of a cross, just an empty cross, and the chain holding it together was unbroken and seemed solid enough. Without a moment's hesitation I placed it round my neck, holding the cross in my hand.

I cannot explain what it was, but having achieved what I had come for, I was now in no rush to leave the chamber at all. I just sat there, for a very long time, deep in thought, and felt I could have stayed there all day, had not my hunger pains got in the way. It was well past normal lunchtime, before I finally decided to go and find the others, in the hope that they had left something for me to eat.

They looked at me curiously when I joined them, but no one asked any questions, and I don't think anyone even noticed my crucifix, as I had tucked it away under my top. This was mine, and mine only, and no one would ever take it away from me. Although I had no idea really what it was, why it was there, and who had placed it where I found it.

The others had finished with the DOG TOWER and the PLUM TOWER already, and only the FOX TOWER remained for that day. But it was all much of a muchness, really. Each tower was mainly built for the defence of the island, and apart from the cannons, which of course the boys enjoyed clambering over and playing with, there was not much to get excited about. We returned home mid-afternoon, and I was the only one who did not look disappointed at all, for I had my treasure. Securely round my neck. I thought to myself that when I go and find that sculpture again, and if that is anything like today, I am a very lucky girl. And I decided there and then that I would tell no one what had already happened and what was still on my mind. The only question was how to convince the others that I had to make a return visit to the BREWERY AND THE BAKERY, where of course is where I first saw the sculpture that so impressed me, and, I remember, impressed THE PRIEST too when I told him about it, although he did not say why.

THE PRIEST? I wonder how he and DAD are getting on, and whether they have reached Christiania yet?

Tuesday, March 19th

A message came by courier this morning, and it was from YULLA and INGRID. The girls confirmed that they had indeed reached Norway, and that the city of Christiania was nearly complete, and that any day now there would be a big opening ceremony and celebration. They also said that longboats from many different countries had arrived in the harbour to be part of the celebrations, and many of the ships had their own priests onboard, who soon came to know and befriend our own PRIEST from Bornholm (I can just imagine how pleased DAD would be about that!)

YULLA and INGRID went on to write that there were no candidates amongst the OARSMEN at all for them to show an interest in. However, amongst the Norwegians there were several tall and handsome, blond men they would quite like to get to know better, so watch this space. They were enjoying themselves anyway.

They finished by writing that DAD had given no indication how long he would want to stay this time. They got the impression that if he continued to be surrounded by PRIESTS and all this talk about God and Jesus, he would probably have had enough sooner rather than later and be on his way home, with or without the rest of us. Good old DAD. The only thing that kept him there was the fact that a few of the crews on the longboats were of the old school, who still put their trust in Odin and Thor. And who agreed with DAD that if all this went on for much longer, there would be an almighty battle between them to see who were right and who were wrong. And he was well prepared for that.

At the end of their letter there was a P.S. saying that some of the visitors to Christiania also had Bornholm in their sights, and that before too long we could expect a good number of boats to enter our harbour. And would we please be kind enough to make Hammershus ready to hold them all, as there was nowhere else on the island, they could think of, to house them. They would probably start arriving in a couple of months' time.

YULLA and INGRID did not mention whether the visitors would be of the Godly kind or favour Odin and Thor, but I guess we are about to find out?

Saturday, March 23rd

I have seen or heard very little of any of the others for a few days now, but I am not too worried. My necklace and I – and I can't stop holding and fondling it – are doing just fine. I guess the others are still disappointed that the three towers did not contain anything worth writing home about. We still have the BUTTER BASEMENT, THE CASTLE BRIDGE and THE CENTRAL FORTRESS to go, of course, and I have my sculpture to revisit too, but none of them know about that one. Anyway, if they want to sulk for a bit, let them. See if I care.

Yesterday another courier arrived with news from Christiania. And imagine my surprise when MUM came to find me, holding a letter addressed to me, and, not only that, from THE PRIEST.

MUM looked as surprised as I felt, but I just took the letter from her, and she did not ask any questions. Later in the day, I went out to find a quiet spot, overlooking the harbour.

"Dear BRITA (or should I call you Princess?") the letter started. "No one knows I am writing this to you, and maybe I shouldn't – DAD would probably kill me, if he knew – but there are things on my heart I need to tell you, BRITA, before it is too late."

I stopped reading for a moment, at once scared and hopeful about what would come next.

"First you need to know that I am not a well man. I wasn't that well when I asked permission to join DAD for Christiania, but this voyage was something I just had to do, while I still can. I am not as young as I used to be, I am not able to spread the Good News about Jesus as much as I want, and I feel there is a long way to go, before the One I believe in will be known to all."

Again, I stopped for a moment and held on to my crucifix, as if somehow doing that would give me courage and strength to read on.

"You see, BRITA, this city, Christiania, has so much possibility in it, and much is good, and many of the folk arriving from so many parts of the world are as keen as I am to make it a Nordic headquarters for Christianity. Why else name it after Christ Jesus himself? However, DAD and others hold different views, and as I am writing this, battle axes are rattling and helmets are being donned, and I fear it will not be long before fighting will erupt, and blood will be spilt."

At this I could read no more but put the rest of the letter away for another day. Before I left my quiet place, I looked across the sea, just in case some of those boats they all talked about were on their way, but no sign of anything. Perhaps they were all too busy preparing for battle in Norway?

I knew that come Monday, MUM would not rest before she had gathered a whole lot of volunteers to get Hammershus ready for all those people, who would soon be arriving, and she would expect us to lend a hand.

With a heavy heart I returned home, feeling sorry for THE PRIEST and wishing so I could read a little further in his letter, but I was not able to. What he wrote about a fierce battle about to start had scared me, although was that not precisely what Vikings often had to be prepared for? Only, this time, it felt different. Who is this battle for – or against? This is what I cannot understand.

Saturday, March 30th

A whole week gone, but Hammershus really does look a lot better now and much more welcoming than ever before. Of course, it is still a ruin, but many of the halls are now covered with timber roofs, to help make those about to come and stay do so in the dry. On this island, we are all determined to show that we welcome everybody and judge no one.

MUM has now suggested that we get the shipyard workers involved in making some proper sleeping quarters at Hammershus for all our visitors too. And she is talking about bunk beds, to pile in as many as possible. At the rate we are going, Hammershus will soon turn into a five-star hotel, rather than an old heap of rocks! She wants all of us to help too as best we can, so I guess I won't have much time to call my troops together for further exploration of the few sites we still have to visit. In fact, I cannot see myself having much time for my Journal in the next few weeks, as by the time we have all done a full day's work, I'll be too tired to write anything.

So, there we are. YULLA and INGRID, we could really do with you here as well. AIFE and RUNE are strong and happy with all the work, but FRIDA, LEIF, LOVA and BJORN are much more reluctant, because they are so much younger and prefer to play. As for me, BRITA, the little Princess, I cannot be seen to take sides. MUM is in charge now, and we must all go and do whatever she says.

Sunday, April 14th

I told you, didn't I? Where has time gone? I must admit, though, I have never seen Hammershus look better. I can only hope that with all this work my sculpture is still intact. I really must get back to it soon and see for myself.

It was only this morning that I remembered I had never finished reading the letter from THE PRIEST. For a while I could not even recall where I had put it last time, but thankfully I found it crumbled up under my pillow, but still easy enough to read. Immediately after breakfast, I returned to my secret and quiet place to try and finish it.

I remembered THE PRIEST writing about a battle he feared was about to start in and around Christiania, and it did not take me long to find the passage where I had left off.

"BRITA," he wrote, "it is not that I fear any battle for myself, it is just that war and fighting seem such a waste of time, and no one really comes out a winner. All I can say is that I am already a winner, for the one I believe in, Jesus, fought my battles for me, died for me, came back to life for me, and lives for evermore. Therefore, I'm a happy man, even though I feel my strength is ebbing away, and I may not have much longer to live on earth."

Here again I had to stop. I never liked it when THE PRIEST talked about dying. Alright, I did not know him that well, but what I did know had always impressed me, and I could not imagine life without him.

"BRITA, it is getting late," he continued in his letter, "and I want to get this message off to you, so I must finish. Before I do, there is something I need to ask you. A favour. When you next go to see the sculpture you told me about, and I know you want to, and you should, promise me that you will go on your own, take your time, sit by it, look at it for a while, see how it might speak to you (although sculptures cannot talk of course) but allow it to enter your heart and mind. You will see what I mean. And before you leave that holy place, for that is what it is, do a bit of digging in the rocks it is standing on, and you may find something which will make everything clearer for you. Thank you, BRITA. And when you have done all this and return home to all the others, I promise you that you will never be quite the same again, nor will those cousins and nephews of yours, when you share with them, as you must do.

I will leave you now. God bless you, BRITA, until we meet again, whenever this may be."

He had signed it with a scribble I could not read, but underneath he had put the name we all knew him by, THE PRIEST.

I put the letter away in my pocket, not quite knowing what to think or say. And so, I didn't think or say anything. I just walked home very quietly.

Wednesday, April 17th

Yesterday we finally got together again, as a group, all seven of us. I felt it had been far too long since we were last able to be ourselves, so we decided to take a picnic this time and head for THE BUTTER BASEMENT. For no other reason than it sounded strange and yet interesting enough to explore. Not that we went expecting much after the disappointment most of my friends had felt about the three towers.

AIFE and RUNE told us that THE BUTTER BASEMENT was so named because many of the taxes paid to the Governor of Hammershus were given in kind rather than money, and good old-fashioned salted Bornholm butter was one of the favourite payment methods. The big containers with all the butter could be kept cool in that basement, so that it would keep fresh until it was exported away from the island. On top of the BUTTER BASEMENT was another battery of cannons known as 'THE CAT'.

My friends and I often wondered where AIFE and RUNE got all their information from, or whether they made it up as they went along, but never mind. Off we went for what we all hoped would be a nice day out.

And it was. It was OK. And I for one was grateful that there was no smell of butter lingering. Most of the large wooden containers were ripped or rotten by now, and there really wasn't a great deal to see of how it must have looked hundreds of years ago. Even the cannons had seen better days and were little more than crumbled black steel, of no use whatsoever.

We had our picnic overlooking the sea. Not at the quiet place only I knew and told no one about, but with good views all the same. And it was as we were packing up that LEIF and FRIDA shouted with one voice, "Look! Ships on the horizon!"

AIFE and RUNE lifted LOVA and BJORN onto their shoulders so that they could see better, while I tried to follow the direction that LEIF and FRIDA pointed, and sure enough, although still a long way from the shore, there were longboats approaching. We could tell from the many beautiful sails that there would be at least half a dozen of them, which could mean that well over a hundred visitors were heading our way.

RUNE estimated that they would be with us in a couple of days at most, depending on the wind (or not). His only concern was that the longboat in front carried a black sail, unlike the boats following behind, where all the sails were colourful and beautifully decorated, as we were used to see them.

A black sail, I thought to myself, and my heart skipped a beat. I knew that black usually spoke of death, and while I tried to say to myself that this could not be, my mind returned to my letter from THE PRIEST, and I just knew there and then that my friend had died and was now on his last journey home.

I did not say anything to the others, but our walk back home was long and mainly quiet, until we saw MUM coming towards us. LOVA and BJORN rushed up to her to tell her that many ships were on their way, and how excited they were about it. DAD was coming home!

"I wonder if YULLA and INGRID have been lucky enough to find a man or two," MUM smiled. "Anyway, we will soon know. Let's go and tell everybody what you have seen on the horizon, not long to wait now."

Saturday, April 20th

All the longboats are now safely anchored in the harbour and absolutely filling it to the brim. We were right about the first boat coming in, the one with the black sails, and we were moved to see how all the other boats kept a respectful distance, until that one was anchored first. Apart from the captain and a couple of foreign priests on that longboat, there was only the body of our very own PRIEST, who would soon be prepared for a Christian burial. Not the normal Viking one, where the PRIEST would have been put to sea in a longboat, and with all his friends ashore setting fire to the boat with burning arrows aimed at it. Nothing is the same anymore. I don't know what is happening.

We did not see THE PRIEST, he was already in his coffin, and the lid was on, perhaps everyone wanted to spare us too much sadness? But once ashore, he was carried all the way up to Hammershus by six strong men and – they tell me – placed in a safe chamber, until such time that the funeral could take place, probably in a week or so.

MUM was thrilled to have DAD back home again, and YULLA and INGRID seemed pleased to see us as well, although they soon let it be known that there were no new men lined up in their lives. I guess they feel no man is good enough for them, they can be so fussy those two.

There were longboats from so many different countries arriving at our small island. We could tell that from the colours and writings on the sails. And we really liked the idea that so many had decided to call in at Bornholm, after having experienced the excitement of the new city of Christiania in Norway first. The only one who did not seem very happy about things was DAD.

It took MUM to get out of him that he was sad and confused about all these new-fangled ideas, and especially all this talk about Jesus. His disappointment was the reason why he called the battle in Norway I mentioned earlier, and which until now we had heard nothing about. MUM pressed DAD about it, and finally he called all nine of us and MUM together and sat us down, so he could tell his story.

"I have never been in such a quick battle before", he started. "My twenty oarsmen were all geared up for it, and we never failed in asking Odin and Thor for power and strength. And yes, we did manage to draw a few more onto our side. But we were completely outnumbered by these Christians and all their talk about their Jesus. They didn't even carry any battle axes or spears, or helmets on their heads. They just came up towards us to meet with us, with outstretched hands and big smiles on their faces. We couldn't believe it. I think each one would have died with a smile on their face, if any of us had threatened to attack."

Here DAD stopped for a short while, deep in thought.

"But we didn't. We couldn't. We might have wanted to, but something stopped us. There were over a hundred of them and just over twenty of us, and in the end, we simply dropped our weapons and expected them to take us prisoners. But they didn't."

Again, DAD was not quite sure how to continue. MUM looked at him, the nine of us looked at him, all wondering where this was going, if anywhere?

"And so," DAD finished, "and so we just all agreed to disagree and sit down and have something to eat and drink, with not a bad word said between us. Just so many smiles and so much laughter. Surely the weirdest battle I have ever been part of. And then, and then, as the party was at its merriest, a messenger came running from the city to say that THE PRIEST had died."

Again, DAD was unable to continue for a long while, but finally he stood up to signal that the meeting was over.

"It took me a while to realize that it was OUR PRIEST they were talking about. That it was MY PRIEST who had died. And I didn't even know he was ill."

Those were DAD's parting words that day, and we all went each our own way quietly.

Saturday, April 27th

It is now Saturday night and well past my normal bedtime really. A whole week has gone without me having time to write anything, nor meet with my friends. We are therefore no further with our last expeditions to THE CENTRAL FORTRESS and THE CASTLE BRIDGE, which really are the only two left to explore. And no, don't worry, I have not forgotten about my private visit to the sculpture and the letter from THE PRIEST, but that will be for me only, and when the time is right. No one else will ever know.

THE CENTRAL FORTRESS and THE CASTLE BRIDGE, on the other hand, will be for all nine of us, I have decided. YULLA and INGRID included, although they are so much older than the rest of us. They are still sulking, because they did not find any men on their trip to Norway, so they need cheering up.

The last week has been busy for all of us islanders in making sure that our visitors have been comfortable in their new accommodation in and around the castle. There have been no complaints, and Mum and her helpers have made sure they always have plenty to eat and drink. How long they intend to stay, we do not know, they seem to have an awful lot to talk about between them in all their different languages. Fortunately, they seem to understand each other well enough most of the time.

They all turned up for the funeral of THE PRIEST, which was this morning. DAD was there too, although he did stay in the background. THE PRIEST was buried near to the BREWERY AND THE BAKERY, where of course the sculpture is hidden, but I did not tell anyone. This is my secret, mine only, and THE PRIEST'S.

The service was taken by two priests, one from Egypt, where of course our PRIEST was picked up by DAD all those years ago, and the other one from the island of Malta in the Mediterranean. That priest spoke to me during the week and told me that one of the followers of Jesus, Paul, who travelled an awful lot after Jesus had died, shipwrecked at Malta. Bue Paul still managed to rescue everybody on that ship and get ashore and gradually get all the Maltesers to believe in Jesus. And they still do, to this day, he said. That's going some, I thought to myself.

Anyway, the service for our dead PRIEST was beautiful. Those who believed in Jesus sang a couple of psalms. There were a couple of readings from something they called Gospels (which they say mean Good News). And a lot of prayer followed, before THE PRIEST was buried deep in the ground, waiting for the day, they said, when he will be risen again, to live with Jesus in Heaven forever.

I could tell DAD was not comfortable with any of this, but he stayed, and then walked quietly home with MUM at the end of it all. Had this been a Viking funeral, everybody would now have found somewhere to eat and drink and be merry long into the night, but here we just all went our separate ways. As the priest from Malta reminded us, "We leave this place with the fondest memories of ANTONIUS in our hearts and minds forever."

ANTONIUS! Now I remembered, this was the name scribbled at the end of the letter from THE PRIEST. I now know his name. I touched the cross, the crucifix, sitting as always round my neck, and it was probably my imagination, but it seemed to have a special glow and certainly felt more precious to me now than ever before.

Tuesday, April 30th

All nine of us finally managed to get together yesterday for a planning meeting. I cannot remember the last time we were able to do that. With all these visitors still with us and occupying so much of the castle grounds with their services and prayer meetings, there is little we can do. However, THE CENTRAL FORTRESS and THE CASTLE BRIDGE remain our priorities.

AIFE and RUNE shared with us that THE CENTRAL FORTRESS was used to defend the entire castle from invaders. Even if those attacking us were lucky enough to get through the outer and inner walls, those defending the castle could find a place of safety here. The central wall was three storeys high and up to two metres thick. It really would take a Goliath or a mountain of a man to get through.

And finally, THE CASTLE BRIDGE, they told us, was the only way to enter or leave the fortress. And the bridge tower had a lookout, from where those defending the castle could keep an eye on those trying to enter, as well as those wishing to leave.

"How much of all this is likely to be left now?", FRIDA asked, "or is it all going to be ruins like everything else we've seen so far? I'm fed up with ruins!" LEIF and LOVE agreed with her. BJORN had no comment to make. He was too young to have an opinion.

"Now, stop moaning, children," said YULLA and INGRID. "It is not AIFE and RUNE's fault that so much has been destroyed. And after all, now that we have all our visitors staying, so much has been, if not restored, at least made more welcoming, don't you think?"

I, BRITA, decided to stay quiet, not wanting to say something about the secret that was only mine. However, as the leader, the PRINCESS, I felt I had to finish the discussion with something positive.

"MUM told me yesterday," I began, "that most of our visitors will be on their way again probably within a week. She also told me that only THE PRIEST from Malta and the PRIEST from Egypt will be staying a little longer, as there are things they still need to do, so they say. I suggest therefore that we meet again as soon as all our guests have departed, and we have waved them goodbye. The two PRIESTS will not get in our way, I promise you that. Let them get on with what they want to do, and I am sure they will let us get on with our adventures. What do you all think?"

Nobody disagreed, and it was left for me to call the next meeting, when the coast was clear.

Monday, May 6th

It's almost three weeks now since our little island was invaded – or should I say visited - by all those people. I have to say they were no trouble, and they have now sailed away to all the corners of the earth, to spread the good news of Jesus. Or so they said. I could tell that DAD for one was glad to see the back of them, he only wished the two PRIESTS from Egypt and Malta had joined them! But they are still here, and I have to say that I quite like especially the one from Malta, and that maybe one day I can find a moment to sit down and have a chat with him, get to know him and his story a little better perhaps?

MUM and many of the farmers on the island have been busy clearing up the castle after the visitors, and the harbour looks very bare now, with only our very own "Golden Explorer" still in dock now that everyone else has left on the other boats. I wonder when DAD will be off on his journeys again, perhaps to see if there is anyone else in the whole wide world who still believe in Odin and Thor?

As for me, I must admit that when we first set out as a group to find Thor's hammer, we were hopeful and convinced that one day we would trace it. Now I am not so sure. It seems that every time we think we may be getting near to something, different items and symbols appear, and there appears to be a real fight going on between the old and the new. Not the kind of fight that DAD likes best, they seem very far between now. I can't remember the last one, the last real Viking battle.

The nine of us decided today that the end of the week will be a good time to start our next adventure. By then most things should be back to normal after the visitors. We agreed to leave for the CENTRAL FORTRESS and the CASTLE BRIDGE on Friday morning, as always well equipped with food and drink.

Saturday, May 11th

I am pleased to say that after the huge disappointment with THE BUTTER BASEMENT (and the three towers before that, remember?) yesterday was very much better and more exciting than we could ever have imagined. And it was early evening before we finally returned home, tired but happy.

Anyway, we entered the CENTRAL FORTRESS by THE CASTLE BRIDGE We could well imagine how in the old days that bridge would be swung open, welcoming those whom the people at the castle wanted to see; but quickly shut with spikes, keeping out those who were not welcome. This was not the first time we crossed the bridge, but it was only now that we quite realized what a wonderful piece of work this must have been.

Once we had arrived in the grounds of THE CENTRAL FORTRESS, we could hardly take in how large it was. On our earlier expeditions we had been too busy trying to get to our various venues, to really understand that this was such a vast area. All the other buildings surrounded this central area, and we simply enjoyed just looking around for a while and then settle down on the grass for something to eat and drink.

This is when the idea came to me to suggest that the others formed small groups and did some exploring without me. They did not need to know that of course I had other plans, but anyway, they all seemed up for it. After some discussion we agreed the following:

YULLA and INGRID (being the two oldest by far) took charge of LOVA and BJORN (the two youngest).

And AIFE and RUNE agreed to look after FRIDA and LEIF.

Group One (YULLA and INGRID's) decided to concentrate on the CASTLE BRIDGE, as we were already there anyway, while Group Two (AIFE and RUNE's) were happy to look at all the outbuildings in the CENTRAL FORTRESS area.

"But what about you, BRITA?", said BJORN with a loud voice. "What will you be doing while we're away?" If looks could kill, he would have died on the spot, but I soon controlled myself and said sweetly, "Don't worry about me. I'm the PRINCESS as you know, and royalty always gets others to do the work for them. Now, off you go, I'll be fine, and I look forward to when you get back and tell me about everything you have found."

They all marched off. It was only when they were completely out of sight that I disappeared into the BREWERY AND THE BAKERY and found my way to the chamber, where I knew the sculpture would be. And it was. And it looked just the same. With the man with the white shining light round his head, and his friends reclining at table, looking at him with so much love and wonder. I touched the necklace and the empty cross, and a wonderful feeling of calm and content came over me, which is difficult to explain.

I remembered my meeting with the PRIEST, when he told me to go again, on my own, and when I felt the time was right to dig a little bit in the soil underneath the sculpture. And yes, I did feel that now the time was right, so I started digging.

Imagine my surprise when soon I came across a piece of papyrus, carefully rolled up, but with my name, yes, **my name**, on the cover. To BRITA, it said, and underneath these words, "with love from ANTONIUS."

The papyrus roll was too large to hide inside my dress, so I quickly emptied out some of the provisions I had in my big holdall and put it in there instead. Now no one would know, and no one could see it and start asking questions. This was mine, and mine only, and I decided there and then to wait for the right time, when again I was on my own, to sit down and read everything.

I also had this funny feeling that it would not be long before I had to arrange a meeting with the PRIEST from Malta. Where that idea came from, I cannot tell, but the feeling was strong. Whether or not I shall also meet with the PRIEST from Egypt, I do not know. After all, they have both stayed behind on our island. There must be a reason why?

Fortunately, I had returned to our meeting point before any of the others arrived back. Once we were all gathered, I asked them, "Well, did anyone find Thor's hammer then? We are running out of places to look."

They had to confess that no, they had no such luck, BUT they had enjoyed a lovely afternoon rummaging through all the old ruins, but without finding anything worth taking home and keeping. I couldn't help smiling and thinking to myself, "Aren't I the lucky one?"

Wednesday, May 15th

It is evening, it is quiet, all my friends have either withdrawn to their rooms or gone to sleep. Tonight is my time to see what my friend THE PRIEST wrote to me, and how on earth he could know that I, of all people, would come across the sculpture AND want to return to find out more. I touched my necklace, and again I had this lovely warm, tingling sensation from the empty cross.

"Dear BRITA," the letter started, "when you read this I shall most likely have gone to a better place, to be with my Father in Heaven. But you must know this: ever since I first saw you, when you came to my services sometimes, and especially when just the two of us met, and I saw you with the crucifix round your neck, I just **knew** that God had plans for you and me. And I just **knew** that Jesus has exciting plans for you, BRITA, even without me. Let me explain.

When DAD picked me up as a prisoner in Egypt all those years ago, and unknown to him, before I became a PRIEST, I was a carpenter and sculptor by trade. One who enjoyed working with wood and other material to make beautiful things out of them. And guess what, BRITA, the unfinished sculpture you have found in the fortress, and which I asked you to go and visit again, is my work. Only, when DAD caught me and took me all the way to Bornholm, I had barely started work on it in my workshop. Yet I managed to get what little I had done into my rucksack and hide it safely on the ship, until we got to your island.

In all the years I have been with you, I have continued to work on the sculpture at the fortress in the darkness of night, with just a few candles to help me see. And where you first saw the sculpture, BRITA, is where I did all the work, unknown to anyone.

You may wonder, in fact, I **know** you wonder what the sculpture is all about. Although I also believe that since you found the crucifix with the empty cross, you are now able to put two and two together. Am I right?"

At this point I put the letter aside. Why was it that THE PRIEST always wrote and spoke things that I could never take in at once, but needed to think long and hard about and then return to later? I looked at the letter and saw that there was still some way to go. I decided that enough was enough for tonight, and soon I was asleep. Not that it was a very solid sleep, as I had so many thoughts milling round in my head...

Monday, May 20th

Now that we seem to have finished exploring the castle together, and certainly without having found any trace at all of Thor's hammer – was there ever such a thing? – all my friends, young and old, seem to be occupying themselves more and more on their own. While in one way that is sad, it is good too, as it gives me, the Princess, much more time to do what I want to do, without having to consult with anyone first.

Yesterday, I went to the church fellowship where I was pleased to see that BOTH PRIESTS were involved in taking the service. I thought maybe this would be my opportunity to make an appointment with the Malta one. You must start somewhere. However, as things turned out, this never happened, as I fell asleep mid-way through the sermon, and I only came to again when I heard people getting up and leaving the building. I felt very embarrassed and sneaked out, hoping that no one had really taken any notice of me, and that I hadn't snored of course.

I decided instead on spending Sunday night catching up with the letter again. My letter from ANTONIUS. And I am so glad I did, for now things began to fall into place.

"BRITA," Antonius had written, "as I write all this to you, I cannot tell what the future will hold. Only God can. However, I do believe that the island of Bornholm, in years to come, will be an important place for Christianity. And I also believe that not so very far from here, a few days' voyage perhaps, a city will be built containing the name of Jesus. And Brita, I think you and all your friends, and MUM and DAD too, will be an important part of what is about to happen. I am only sorry I will probably not be around to see it or hear about it."

Here I stopped for a moment, to let it all sink in. How could THE PRIEST have known about Norway and Christiania even then, while he was still working on his sculpture? So many years before it all began to happen?

I picked up the letter again, to finish reading it. "Finally, BRITA, you may wonder what my sculpture is all about when you find it, as I just know you will. So, let me explain. The man with the halo, or shining light, is Jesus, and the men with him are his disciples. They are sharing in bread and wine, in a very special meal called Holy Communion. And one day, BRITA, you will know what that is all about. And you will want to share it with all your friends and with all the adults on the island as well. Just one more thing. At some point, as Bornholm gets on the Jesus map – just wait and see – you may find other PRIESTS arriving. As and when they do, promise me that you will meet with them, for they will have stories to tell just as exciting as mine. God bless you, BRITA, I must try and get this sculpture finished, while there is still time."

Friday, May 24th

All my friends came to find me yesterday, and they were not happy. None of them were. In fact, they were furious with me.

AIFE and RUNE were the first to tear into me. "BRITA," they said, "we haven't seen you out and about for over a week. The little ones are missing you like mad, and some of us older ones too. You are keeping yourself to yourself far too much, and we are very worried about you. Have we done anything to upset you?"

For just a moment I did not know what to say. Not surprisingly, LOVA and BJORN, being the youngest, also seemed to be the saddest looking. I enfolded them in my arms for a big hug and a kiss. AIFE and RUNE, far too old for this kind of thing, flew to the end of the queue, sharply followed by YULLA and INGRID, probably still moaning about their failure to find any husbands on their recent voyage. Which left FRIDA and LEIF, who were still young enough to remember the power of a good, long cuddle.

After a while, the four of us let go of each other, and by then I had thought of something to say to the others.

"I am sorry," I started, "I've had a lot on my mind, but that is no excuse. What with the PRIEST dying, and then discovering that he had written a long letter especially to me, while he was working on something special at the castle. And then there's the crucifix I found and never told you about. Not to mention DAD in such a bad mood, wanting to talk to me, but never yet got round to it. And MUM so busy with all the people from so many different countries, who have not long gone. And all the strange things I have heard about at church on a Sunday, when I can stay awake that is. It has been too much for me all at once. Perhaps I should have shared much more with the rest of you, rather than keeping everything to myself? I am sorry."

"Okay, then," said AIFE, "what are you going to do about it, to make it up to us?"

This is when I remembered the words of the PRIEST, when he asked me to share his sculpture with all my friends, and indeed show it to them. "Perhaps just one more visit to the BREWERY AND THE BAKERY is in order? There is something there I have kept to myself all this time. And after that I would like us all to go and talk to the PRIEST FROM MALTA, which is something else I promised to do."

YULLA and INGRID looked truly puzzled at this. Which was strange, as they were the only ones who attended church at least sometimes, so they would know him. After a little while, they both nodded and YULLA said, "Perhaps best if just the three of us go and see the PRIEST to start with, BRITA. You know what DAD thinks about all this, and I am not sure where MUM stands on it. For us all to go is not a good idea, at least not to start with."

I could only agree, so I closed the meeting by saying, "OK, then. As I said, I really am sorry about everything. Let us find a good time, and soon, to return to my secret chamber at the BREWERY AND THE BAKERY. All of us together. Agreed?"

They all nodded, and we decided to meet again in a day or two to set a date.

Tuesday, May 28th

That meeting never happened! MUM and DAD got hold of me a couple of days ago, saying, "BRITA, we need to have a serious talk, and we have asked YULLA and INGRID to join us too." My heart sank, but there was nothing I could say or do, so the meeting took place last night, with just the five of us present.

MJM started off, which was highly unusual, as up to now all meetings were called and led by me, being the Princess! I had to swallow my pride and stay calm, but it wasn't easy.

"DAD and I," MUM started, "have noticed with much concern that you have spent far too much time away on your own, OR with one of the PRIESTS, recently. We need to remind you who you are, where you are, and what you are."

I said nothing, waiting for MUM, or maybe someone else, to continue. YULLA and INGRID said nothing, they just sat there with their eyes towards the floor.

It was DAD who took up the challenge from MUM. "BRITA," he said, "you know we love you, and always shall. You are our little Viking Princess, and you always will be. However, since I came back from Norway, it seems to me that you are causing a lot of confusion and sadness around our island, with all your Jesus talk and meetings with the PRIEST. At least until he died, Odin and Thor keep him safe. This is upsetting, to me not least, and it needs to stop.

We are Vikings, never forget, we were born Vikings and we shall die Vikings, whenever our gods so desire. Anything else is fantasy and a waste of time. Do you hear what I'm saying?"

I had to give credit to DAD. He had not once raised his voice, which was unusual for him. I always preferred DAD when he was a bit angry, at least you knew where you stood with him. Now I wasn't quite sure, so, taking a deep breath, I took my chance.

"DAD, I am sorry for any wrongdoing I have been guilty of, but I have to say also that I cannot promise to completely ignore everything I have learnt and heard about over so many months. In fact, I promised THE PRIEST not to keep things to myself, but to share them with my cousins and nephews, and with you and MUM too. And I promised him also that I would continue my discussions with the PRIEST from MALTA, who is now staying with us, and so I shall. However, I do know I'm a Viking, I do know I'm your Little Princess, I do know that Odin and Thor mean a lot to so many people here. But I also know that there is something and someone else I need to learn about. And share with those I come across. And I shall. And no one can stop me."

I don't think I have ever in my young life spoken for so long, and I needed to write it all down in my Journal, lest I forget.

Perhaps I expected an uproar? Perhaps deep down I wanted DAD to fly at me, so we could get this over with and start with a clean sheet? But none of that happened. DAD looked at me sadly, took MUM by the hand and quietly left the room. YULLA and INGRID stayed with me for a few minutes, then they got up, and only now had this to say, "A fine mess you've made of this, BRITA. You wait. If you think you've got away with it, you have another thing coming. Perhaps not immediately, but when you least expect it." And with that they left me, with my own thoughts to commit to my Journal.

Friday, May 31st

There is a lot of activity in the drydock. Not only is "Golden Explorer" undergoing a facelift – again – but some of the older longboats in the fleet are being taken out of their mothballs, and, it seems to be, made ready for action. DAD is supervising all the work, but he is keeping totally quiet about what exactly is going on. I guess MUM will have some idea, but he is not saying a word to me or any of my friends, not that I know of anyway.

Yesterday I found my own little hiding place overlooking the harbour, and if I counted correctly, I think about twenty longboats, large and small, are being dragged out and prepared. This could mean that a few hundred warriors may soon be ready to set sail, commandeered by DAD, I have no doubt.

What are they up to? I wonder if the PRIEST from MALTA might know, although I do not think he and DAD have much, if anything, to say to each other. I could try and find out, though. If I go to church on Sunday, perhaps he can spare me a few minutes after the service? It's worth a try.

I have not seen much of my friends since Tuesday, despite my best intentions. I wonder if they too wonder what is happening in the drydock and harbour. Or is it only me? After all, getting the boats ready and setting sail is nothing unusual; only this time it does not look like just any old voyage, more like a full-blown exercise, if you ask me, and I fear it could all get a bit violent. Will I ever know?

Monday, June 3ʳᵈ

The PRIEST from MALTA did appreciate seeing me at church, and in fact, once he had bid farewell to all the worshippers that morning, he invited me to join him in the vestry inside the church. Unusually, he locked the door, so that we would not be disturbed.

He started by looking at me seriously, before shaking his head and almost in a whisper saying, "BRITA, oh BRITA, it is not going to plan, is it? Nothing is..."

I did not know what to reply and decided just to wait for him to continue, when he was ready.

"You see, BRITA," he said finally, "I have been waiting a long time for this moment, and I really do think you could have made the effort to come and see me sooner. I also think you could have taken your little friends to see the sculpture that I know you found, and which your friend, THE PRIEST, wanted them all to see with you. Why haven't you?"

Again, I was at a loss for words, didn't know what to say. How could he know what THE PRIEST had written in his letter to me. How could he know that he, the PRIEST from MALTA, was one I had particularly been asked to talk to? I couldn't make sense of it.

"And now it is getting late, BRITA, and it is getting dangerous too. You have no doubt observed all the activity in the drydock and harbour over the last few days. And perhaps wondered what is going on? Well, let me tell you this: DAD is on the warpath, he's had enough of me and all my Jesus talk, and of you not behaving like his Viking Princess at all. He is about to set out on the most important journey of his life. He is planning to take a couple of hundred warriors with him. And do you know where they are heading, BRITA? Have you guessed?"

It was then that it came to me. How could I not have guessed? The truth was staring me in the face right there and then. "Norway!", I whispered, "Christiania. He's returning with force to sort out all those Christians once and for all, isn't he? And there'll be an almighty battle, won't there? People may die..."

The PRIEST from MALTA looked at me sadly, then nodded his old head. "I reckon they'll be ready to set off in a couple of weeks' time myself. So, we haven't got long..."

"But what can we do to stop it?", I said.

At this he took my hand in his and said, "We can but pray, BRITA. Pray for a peaceful end to all this, for I have no doubt that we will not be able to stop the ships from going. But what we can do, you and I and all your friends, and I mean ALL your friends, is to find our way back to the sculpture. There you can share with them what it means to you, and I can perhaps share what I know too. How does that sound?"

"So, there will be a battle?" I said with a shiver in my voice. "No matter what we do or don't do?" "Yes, I think so," he replied, "but we can all meet and pray by the sculpture that something good will come of it. We can do no more, but we should do no less."

At this, I hugged the old PRIEST and promised him that I would explain to all my friends how urgent it was for us to return with him to Hammershus and finally begin to understand what was going on. What battles were taking place, not forgetting the one soon to come. "It's all to do with Jesus beating Odin and Thor, isn't it?" I said, not knowing where it came from, but I was relieved finally to see a big smile on his face as I got up and left.

Monday, June 10th

A whole week gone, and where do I start?

Following my meeting with THE PRIEST, it did not take me long to gather all my friends and explain what now had to happen, and quickly. Last Wednesday, we were all on the march back to Hammershus and my secret place containing the sculpture. I made sure to wear my crucifix, as I had this strange but wonderful feeling that there was a power coming from it, which I could not explain, but which felt very real.

It was quite easy for us to get away unnoticed, as MUM and DAD were all busy with their two hundred or so warriors down at the shipyard. Getting everything ready for their voyage. Yes, MUM was going to join them this time, as she felt it would be much easier to cook meals for them all onboard day by day, than try to prepare a shipload in advance to last the whole journey.

We lost BJORN a couple of times on the way, until AIFE decided to have mercy on him and carry him the last bit. FRIDA and LOVA too got tired towards the end, so YULLA and INGRID took hold of one each to help them along. Which left RUNE, LEIF, and me, BRITA to lead the gang together with THE PRIEST. Who, despite his old age, was surprisingly nimble on his feet, and, it seemed to me, eager to get there.

We finally arrived at THE BREWERY AND THE BAKERY, and I was relieved to see that the sculpture was where it had always been, in one piece, and with the sunlight on it almost inviting us in. I heard YULLA and INGRID gasp, as they let go off FRIDA and LOVA, and they fell on their knees in front of the sculpture. I could not believe my eyes, those two of all people, always so sceptical of everything I did, or should I say did not do.

RUNE and AIFE shook their heads as if to ask what all the fuss was about. LEIF, BJORN, FRIDA AND LOVA were all too young to really understand, but they were happy to come and join me and THE PRIEST in our small circle. With most of the older ones sitting down near us, and yet at a safe distance, just in case. Except for FRIDA and LOVA, who were still on their knees. If I did not know better, it almost looked as if they prayed...

THE PRIEST spoke first. For most of them this was the first time they met him or heard him talk, as they never went to church on a Sunday, but his voice was loud and clear, and he soon had all our attention.

"Before we have a close look at the sculpture," he began, "let me share with you what happened on the island I come from, Malta, almost a thousand years ago. Have any of you heard about the apostle PAUL?"

All my friends shook their heads, no surprise there, but I remembered vaguely THE PRIEST having mentioned the name in one of his sermons. I did not say anything, though.

"Well, PAUL was one of many early followers of Jesus, who did great things and helped spread the word of Jesus throughout the world as it was then. And from there to places like Norway and yes, Bornholm, as we have it today. He was an apostle, and he suffered many spells in prison and many dangers, as he travelled the world, all because of his trust in Jesus."

None of us said anything but waited for the old man to continue.

"One year, on one of his voyages, and this one on the way to Rome, where he was to be imprisoned, the ship he was on got stuck on the rocks in the most awful storm. Everyone onboard thought they were going to die and that the ship would surely sink. PAUL, because of his faith and trust in Jesus, prayed to God, and helped everyone get safely to shore. Here they were met by the natives of MALTA, which is where the ship had stranded. And over the next few years, PAUL helped the whole population of that island come to believe in Jesus as well."

FRIDA and LOVA only now stood up and walked nearer to THE PRIEST, where he and I and the little ones made room for them within our little circle. Neither of them said anything, just sat quietly with us.

"And this Jesus, who meant so much to Paul, and who came to mean everything to my own people in Malta, and to me not least, he is the same Jesus who is now becoming known in Norway and yes, in Bornholm, and I want to tell you about him."

RUNE and AIFE now also approached our circle, and soon we were all sat together, side by side, preparing to hear what THE PRIEST wanted to share with us. I will stop here but continue tomorrow, as there is so much to remember and take in.

Tuesday, June 11th

"This sculpture, which BRITA found," sad THE PRIEST, "was started by your very own Priest, who was with you long before I came. The one whom DAD caught in Egypt and then brought all the way to Bornholm. And the same one who died on DAD's first trip to Norway, and whom we buried quite close to where we find ourselves now. You remember?"

We all nodded, oh yes, we remembered.

"Well, as you can see, he never quite finished what he was working on; but there is enough here for me to share a thing or two with you, if you please?"

I looked at my friends, and I was pleased to see that none of them seemed in any hurry to get up and go; not even those who were anything but keen when we first set out.

With nothing or no one to stop him, THE PRIEST continued, "You see before you Jesus, the one all in white and with a halo round his head. Surrounded by twelve men, seated, or should I say reclining, at a large table with cups and plates on it. You will have to look closely, but it is all there."

THE PRIEST allowed us to get up and draw nearer and study for ourselves, as he continued, "What you see is Jesus sharing in a simple meal with his best friends, the night before he is caught by Roman soldiers and imprisoned, to suffer a cruel and painful death. On a cross."

I nodded as I had often heard THE PRIEST speak about this in his sermons, but I did wonder how many, if any, of the others knew what he was talking about.

"So, on the night before he was taken away by the soldiers, and remember, he knew all along this would happen, he needed and wanted to share this special time with his loved ones. And therefore, he took bread, blessed it, broke it, and passed it round to each one of them. Later he took the cup of wine, blessed it and passed that round too for everyone to have a sip. When they had all received, he said to them, "The next time I share in the bread and the wine will be with my Father in Heaven."

At hearing this, I could see some of my older friends becoming a little uneasy and fidgety, but they did not prepare to get up and move. They stayed with the rest of us.

"You see, Jesus knew all along what would happen. He knew he would have to suffer, but he also knew that his death on the cross would not be the end. He knew that God would raise him again to live, and more than that, to live for evermore. He prepared this meal for his friends to prepare them for when he would no longer be with them for a while. And to help them continue to spread the good news of him to the whole world, namely that he, Jesus, was not only a human being like them, but more, much more than that. He was the Son of God."

Here THE PRIEST had to stop, and we could see that he was exhausted. I felt I had to say something, while he got his breath back.

"It seems to me," I started, "that there is something important about the sculpture not being quite finished! It is as if those few missing bits are those that we need to put in ourselves, when we are ready to believe. Am I right?"

The old man smiled and said, "BRITA, you are very wise for your age. While I am sure THE PRIEST would have liked to finish his work, I believe there is a lot of truth in what you say. It is only when we can put in our own belief, and heart and soul that it is all complete."

There was a long pause, before INGRID said this which I will remember for as long as I live. "And now DAD is preparing to go to war in Norway against those who believe in Jesus. And we don't know how it is all going to work out. But one thing I do know. YULLA and I came to this place, and we were both struck by the moment and by what we saw. Even before anyone spoke, we had to kneel and quietly pray. And now I think there is nothing more important for us all to do, right here and now, than to kneel and pray."

I could see THE PRIEST becoming quite overwhelmed at this, but before he or anyone else could respond, it was BJORN, our youngest member, who brought us all back to earth. "Yes," he shouted out loud, "Let us all kneel and pray that Jesus will beat Odin and Thor, and that DAD too will come to understand. And can we also pray that not too many lives will be lost in battle, but that most of our people will come home safely."

None of us could quite believe that such a young person could have so much wisdom in his head, but we all knelt and folded our hands in that circle, while THE PRIEST led us in prayer.

Friday, June 14th

Something really has changed since our visit with THE PRIEST to the sculpture. And for the better too. It is hard to explain, but whenever we get together now, which we do a lot, all nine of us - whether it is to play or read or plan our next adventure - we always start with a prayer. And not only that, but we take it in turns to lead. I have always been so used to being the one everybody expects to lead everything, but this is so much better. Everyone gets their turn, and BJORN, so young, keeps surprising us with his wise words.

Yesterday we even decided, all of us, that we would go and listen to THE PRIEST on Sunday morning. We did not even refer to him as our priest from Malta anymore, he was simply our very own PRIEST now. For just a moment we felt that perhaps we ought to let MUM and DAD know about this, but seeing how busy they still were down in the docks, we decided they had enough on their minds. We could always tell them afterwards.

Sometimes, when we meet, it feels strange at first to pray to Jesus and not to call on Odin and Thor, as we had been used to doing for so many years. However, we all agreed that the name of Jesus had such a wonderful and calming ring to it which we had never known before. How I wish MUM and DAD and their hundreds of warriors would come to know also. Perhaps I should pray about that?

Monday, June 17th

Yesterday afternoon, after the service at church and lunch, and while I was resting in my chamber, there was a knock on my door. Without waiting for me to answer, DAD and the PRIEST from MALTA suddenly stood in the middle of the room. You could have knocked me down with the feather. The two of them – together? Unheard of.

DAD started the conversation. "BRITA," he began, "the PRIEST and I have talked and agreed that perhaps it would be a good idea for you, my little Princess, and him to come along when we head towards Norway in just a few days' time. What do you think of that idea, BRITA?"

I could hardly believe my ears, but my first thought went to those I'd be leaving behind. "What about all my friends? And what about church if the PRIEST comes too?" At this, the PRIEST took my hand and said reassuringly, "Don't worry about church, BRITA. The PRIEST from EGYPT will stay here and look after that side of things. He will also care for all your friends. Not forgetting YULLA and INGRID, AIFE and RUNE who will keep a close eye on the younger ones. DAD and I have already discussed and agreed that with them."

I felt reassured and almost wanted to jump with joy, but one look at DAD and I soon controlled myself. "Just one word of warning, BRITA," he said, "All this does not mean that I am suddenly onboard with you and the PRIEST and all your young friends, when you go on about this Jesus business. Not at all. And me and my men are not heading for Norway in peace, but to show them over there a thing or two about Odin and Thor, and what they mean to us! Never forget that."

Out of the corner of my eye I saw the PRIEST wink at me, but at the same time his eyes were clearly telling me not to argue with DAD, but for now quietly accept what DAD was saying. Therefore, I just nodded and took DAD's hand in mine.

"I'd love to come, DAD, and thank you for asking me. I promise you and MUM not to get in the way of anything. And now you must both excuse me, I need to start packing!"

Thursday, June 20th

I can hardly believe that we are finally on our way to Norway! All being well, we should arrive at Christiania in the next week to ten days or so, but we all know what the weather can be like on the crossing. I must say that seeing all these beautiful ships heading the same way, with their sails in full flow, is a sight to behold, or you could almost say for the gods to behold.

I spent most of yesterday, having finished packing the day before, bidding farewell to all my friends and giving them final instructions. Such as don't forget to write, and don't forget church on a Sunday. I also reminded them that we had still not managed to find any trace of Thor's hammer, and whether perhaps they ought to make another excursion to the Hammershus ruin? Most important, I told the younger ones that YULLA and INGRID, AIFE and RUNE were in charge and had to be obeyed at all times.

Little BJORN had the last word. "But how do we know that our letters will reach you, BRITA? There's an awful lot of water between here and Norway. And will you have time to write back to us?"

I gave him a big cuddle and LOVA, FRIDA and LEIF too. They were so young, and I found it hard to leave them behind. After all, they were so used to their little Princess to sort everything out for them. "Don't worry," I said, "just stick your notes in a bottle, put the cork on tight, and chuck it in the sea addressed to us. It will get to where we are, you just wait and see."

Sunday, June 23rd

The PRIEST from MALTA conducted a service on the open deck of the Golden Explorer this morning. After all, ours was the biggest and the finest of the boats and always leading the rest across the ocean. It was impossible to get everyone who wanted to onboard the one ship, but we managed to steer the other boats as close as possible to the Golden Explorer. This way all those, who wanted to, could hear what was being said. Things always carry so clearly when you are on water.

DAD decided that he was having none of this and disappeared below deck for the half hour the service lasted, and about half of his men followed him. The other half stayed behind, and some fell on their knees, ready for prayer, while most just sat or stood around and waited expectantly, MUM included.

I looked across to the other longboats alongside us, and it was the same there. Half the crews disappeared below deck, with the other half staying on deck, and I wondered what all this meant, and what the PRIEST would be thinking.

The half hour seemed to go very quickly. I cannot remember everything THE PRIEST said or prayed about, but I did notice that some of the oarsmen, soon to become warriors (if DAD had his way) had tears in their eyes when he finished, and before they got back to work.

MUM sat quietly at the back for a little while, before going downstairs to fetch DAD, assuring him that the PRIEST had finished, and it was safe to continue the journey. "About time," DAD muttered, "I don't know what to make of all this Jesus lark, perhaps I should have left him at home! The PRIEST I mean…"

I decided to stay quiet, but in my heart of hearts I was so glad that the PRIEST was onboard.

Wednesday, June 26th

A week almost gone, and today is the first time we sail into bad and stormy weather. We are over half-way to Christiania, but the storm we are heading into now will surely delay us. The oarsmen keep doing their best against the elements, but it isn't easy for them. DAD is struggling in making himself heard and get them to follow his instructions. MUM has gone downstairs, partly because she is feeling just a little seasick, but I notice that the PRIEST is sitting calmly at the stem. Just rocking and moving gently in tune with the waves. I decide to go and join him. DAD frowns, but he says nothing.

Thursday, June 27th

The stormy weather continued all night, but this morning everything is much brighter and calmer again. "I think we only have another three or four days to go," says DAD, satisfied that Odin and Thor have looked after us all so well through the danger. As for me, I think Jesus had as much a hand in things, if not more, but I would never dare upset DAD.

Friday, June 28th

Oh dear, it seems that we celebrated too soon yesterday, thinking we had weathered the storm so well. When night set in, it soon became clear that some of the longboats had been damaged and were falling badly behind the mothership, Golden Explorer. DAD was getting very impatient, as he had to accept that his fleet would not now reach Christiania as one unit and all at once, but by and by. And he could only stand on the bridge and look forlorn, as he watched many of the oarsmen in the smaller boats reduced to making necessary repairs whenever the sea was calm and rowing not essential. At one point the PRIEST walked up and stood beside him. What they talked about, I could not hear, but it wasn't long before DAD turned and walked away, looking very unhappy. As I am writing this, some of the boats are so far behind now that we can barely see them. I wouldn't be surprised if some of the captains on those decide to call it a day and return to Bornholm.

Sunday, June 30th

Not much changed yesterday, if anything it got worse, and by the time we could see the Norwegian coast and the bay of Christiania in the distance, there were only five boats left out of the original twenty or so. I heard DAD say that perhaps he shouldn't be surprised knowing how old and badly looked after those old plimsolls had been! "Good riddance to them!", I heard him shout, "we won't miss them, we'll be okay, we're still just under a hundred men left, we'll show those Norwegians what for!" And when MUM joined him soon after, she said sweetly, "And of course there's more food left for the rest of us!" She was right. While we had been a full fleet, a lot of time and effort had been taken up with getting provisions from Golden Explorer in small boats across to the other vessels. No more of that now. DAD was pleased.

Early this morning, he called us all together, after having sent one messenger across to the four boats alongside us, so that each captain and crew would get the same information at the same time. And this is what DAD had to say.

"We'll be ashore on Tuesday morning. And I want us to dock with all guns blazing and swords raised, ready for battle. We do not come in peace, we come as warriors, protected by Odin and Thor, to claim this new land. I want all of you to fight hard, even to death, except for MUM and BRITA, of course, who will stay on Golden Explorer and wait for us to return."

"But what about the PRIEST?", I ventured. "Ha! The PRIEST! What about the PRIEST! He'll come along with us. He won't need full armour, of course, he thinks he is already protected by his good Lord Jesus! HA!" At this DAD laughed out loud and some of his men followed suit, but not all. Some bowed their heads, as if in prayer, and looked at the PRIEST rather than at DAD. As for the PRIEST, he just stood there, saying nothing, but with his head held high and his eyes lifted towards heaven.

Wednesday, July 3rd

I shall never forget yesterday for as long as I live. All the men standing on the decks of the five remaining ships, battle ready, with their swords lifted high, their visors protecting their faces, helmets on their heads, and the full armour covering their bodies. And, as Golden Explorer was the first to birth, DAD fired three shots from the cannon to warn the people on the shore what was about to hit them. Literally.

But this is where I got confused. For where was the opposing army? Where were all the Norwegians who surely, surely, would want to come and see what this was all about and protect their country. I could not see anyone on the vast stretch of sand, not a single person for as far as the eye could see.

"HA!" said DAD. "They are probably all asleep still. It is early morning, after all." And so it was, barely 5 a.m. DAD always believed in attacking nice and early, whenever he ventured to a new country. Sometimes it worked, sometimes not.

"Anyway, that won't stop us! On my orders, we set foot ashore, and we march, and we march for as long as it takes, until those sleepyheads begin to realize they are in serious trouble. And by then, it will be too late. We have the element of surprise."

But before DAD could give the order, the PRIEST stood by him again and quietly pointed across the dunes. There in the sunrise we could now all see hundreds of people, not just men, but women and children among them, slowly but surely walking, not running, whispering, not shouting, come ever nearer to us, who had not even left our boats yet. Taken completely by surprise we were, even DAD looked bewildered.

As the crowd drew nearer, a giant of man walked ahead and soon he was face to face with DAD and the PRIEST. He really was a very tall man, taller than DAD and the PRIEST for sure. He had blond hair and piercing blue eyes, but he was completely unarmed and went up to the two men with his arms outstretched.

"Welcome to Christiania," he said. "On behalf of all of Norway, welcome to our new city, named after Jesus Christ, our Lord and Saviour. Come on and follow me, all of you. You must be starving!"

Saturday, July 6th

It has taken me a few days to return to my Journal. There is so much happening, and so quickly, that it is hard to take it all in.

We walked along the beach and in between the dunes for what seemed ages, before we came to a clearing with the most fantastic open-air meal laid out for us. Never have I seen so much delicious food. Even MUM had a job taking it all in and clasped her hands together in utter amazement.

Our host – and we still did not know his name, but he seemed to be their leader – asked THE PRIEST if he would offer a grace on the meal, which of course he gladly did, much to DAD's annoyance. And the tall giant of man then asked the Vikings if they might not be more comfortable without all that extra armour to weigh them down? "You must be most uncomfortable," he said. They looked at DAD for permission, which he reluctantly gave, and soon all the armour formed a great big pile in the sand. The men then sat down to eat.

At the end of the meal, the tall, blonde Norwegian suggested to them that now they had come prepared to fight, and instead of a lot of blood being spilt, perhaps they might like to entertain their hosts to a pretend Viking battle the next day, after a good night's sleep? But without killing anyone, of course, just acting out for us all to enjoy. Again, the oarsmen com warriors looked at DAD, and again, with a deep sigh, he surrendered. I looked at THE PRIEST, and not surprisingly he had a job containing himself. This was just up his street.

And so, the next day, the fiercest but pretend Viking battles ever seen took place on that beach, and again the day after. The Norwegians just loved it, and they applauded DAD's men in acting everything out. Not only that, but on the third day most of the boats that had been damaged in the storm and – we thought – were returning home, suddenly appeared on the horizon and came to re-join us. Making the battles even longer and fiercer, but always without a single drop of blood being shed.

Monday, July 8th

Yesterday we had an open-air service on the beach, led jointly by our PRIEST and the tall, blonde Norwegian, whose name we still did not know. I guess because no one had asked him, or perhaps no one thought it really mattered. We must have been about three hundred people on that beach. It was lovely to share bread and wine with one another, before at lunchtime we enjoyed yet another big three course dinner.

I don't think I have ever eaten so much in my life, and MUM did not have to do a thing. The Norwegians saw to everything and made us feel so welcome. There was no big battle being enacted on the Sunday. As the PRIEST and the tall Norwegian both agreed, Sunday is a day of rest. However, we can have another battle tomorrow and the next day, and for as long as you want to stay, for we really enjoy seeing you Vikings battle it out! DAD muttered something, I'm not sure what, it didn't sound very nice, but none of his men seemed to mind the arrangements and suggestions being made.

Wednesday, July 10th

Yesterday, finally, we were all invited to come and see the city and everything it had to offer, so we left the beach and followed our leader. We were surprised at the beauty and the peace of Christiania, even with so many people milling about. There seemed to be no rushing around of any kind, everyone we met were good-natured and welcoming. The churches we visited were plain but big and airy, and we immediately felt at home. Some of DAD's men even knelt at the altar, and the PRIEST offered to pray with anyone who wanted it. It was a time of such harmony and love, and more than once did I wish that all my friends were here with me, instead of probably being bored stiff in Bornholm. I had not heard anything from them, nor did I really expect to, but I thought about them – often.

Friday, July 12th

We have been here almost a week and a half now, and I can tell that DAD is getting impatient. Nothing has really gone the way he had hoped and expected, and it was easy to see that he was keen to return home. He spoke to MUM and the PRIEST, and they agreed between them that we would have one more weekend with the Norwegians and then set sail on the Monday morning. The Norwegians were thrilled, as this meant they could enjoy a few more Viking battles on their sandy beach.

I am writing this at night-time, but it was this afternoon, after probably the fiercest battle yet, we saw DAD and the PRIEST walk up to the tall Norwegian together and sit down with him in the dunes. I know I probably should not have done it, but I followed them at a safe distance without them knowing. I hid in a big dune, far enough away for them not to see me, yet close enough for me to hear every word they said.

DAD started the conversation. "I have to be honest," he said, "I came here with my men expecting to completely take over Christiania and keep as prisoners anyone we did not kill. I was all prepared to fight the fiercest battle of my life, under the guidance of Odin and Thor, in whom I trust and believe. But now…"

Here DAD seemed overwhelmed with emotion, and the PRIEST took his hand and held it at his heart.

"But now I just do not know anymore. I have met with such friendliness and love, more than anywhere else in my life, and I cannot understand it." He looked at the Norwegian. "Why do none of you fear us or hate us or keep away from us, knowing that we came with no good intentions at all? You must have known."

The tall Norwegian looked at DAD with his piercing blue eyes and took hold of his other hand, saying words I shall never forget. "When you arrived, I could tell that you were ready for battle. But I could also tell that fierce fighting was not the only battle raging in your heart. And I, we, decided to come to you in love and hospitality instead of armed with weapons, as we could so easily have done. After all, there are far more of us than there are of you."

DAD looked at him, begging him to continue.

"I could soon tell that the battle you and many of your men were fighting was the battle in your hearts and minds trying to decide whether Odin and Thor really are the greatest. Or whether there is someone greater still. And now, as you prepare to leave on Monday, I think you know."

The Norwegian and the PRIEST now stood up in that sand, and DAD did too, and they all held hands, and the PRIEST offered this prayer, "Lord Jesus, bless DAD for being prepared to be surprised by the love and generosity of these people, whose city bears your name. And help him on our homeward journey to sit quietly with MUM and his men and share what he has found here for himself, so that they too will find, and believe. Amen."

After a brief pause, The Norwegian asked DAD, "Time for one more final battle tomorrow afternoon, do you think?"

With tears in his eyes, DAD looked at him and said, "No, I think we have battled enough already. What time is the service on Sunday? Can I come? And invite MUM and my men?"

I did not hear the answer, but I guessed what it would be. I was too busy trying to get away from them, out of sight, lest they saw me.

I can write no more. It is getting late, and my eyes are tired.

Tuesday, July 16th

Yesterday was another one of those I shall never forget for as long as I live. MUM and DAD had decided that it would be wise to set sail and get going at daybreak. But even at that early hour, all the Norwegians, who had been there welcoming us almost two weeks ago, were there again, seeing us off. All, that is, except one…

DAD noticed it too and many of his men. "Where is their chieftain," they asked around, "the tall white chap with the piercing blue eyes who seemed so much in control? Surely, he was their leader?"

One of the women in the group laughed out loud and said, "Oh, you mean ERLING? Don't wait for him, I tell you, as you might still be here in a month's time. ERLING comes and goes as he wills. In fact, I have never known him stay for anyone for a whole two weeks before. You should feel honoured."

MUM and DAD looked at each other. How strange? Surely a chieftain, a leader, was always there, where it mattered most, how could he not now be on that beach? Leaving it to everybody else?

I saw the PRIEST trying hard not to smile, as if there was something he knew only too well, but wanted to keep for himself, for now anyway.

I thought no more of it then, busy as I was with everybody else to get everything loaded back on the ships for the return journey. And in my heart, although I had very much enjoyed Christiania and learned a lot from the experience, I could not wait to get back and see all my friends again! Every one of them, from the oldest, YULLA and INGRID, AIFE and RUNE, to the youngest, FRIDA and LEIF, LOVA and BJORN, the smallest of them all. Not long now, and we would be back to see them on the shore waving us in. I was sure of it.

However, as we set sail and all those people on the shore waved us goodbye, I still could not help asking myself where that man was, the one they called ERLING? Strange, coming and going like that...

Friday, July 19th

Two full days and nights at sea already, and the weather is behaving itself. Not only the weather! DAD is a different person! Every morning at daybreak, he signals to all the ships to draw together and form one very large circle with the 'Golden Explorer' right bang in the middle. But of course! She always will be DAD's pride and joy, and it is from her deck that he and the PRIEST will conduct a sunrise service together every morning to set the tone for the day. And ask God – yes, God! – for good weather. I could not believe my ears. What had happened to Odin and Thor?

Yesterday DAD even pointed out to all the sailors that by forming a circle and with him and the PRIEST in the middle, everybody could be heard. This was how water carried sound. And he went on to say that God knew this, because often he sent his Son Jesus onto the water to speak to people on the shore, knowing that they would all be able to hear. I could but listen and try to take it all in. Just wait till we get back to Bornholm, and I can share this with all my friends.

Monday, July 22nd

Already a week at sea, and all is good. Much better in fact than the voyage across to Norway. At this rate, we might even reach Bornholm a day early.

Yesterday being Sunday, the service was longer than the usual sunrise ones, and DAD even allowed the PRIEST to preach a sermon, "as long as you don't rabbit on too long!" as he said to him with a twinkle in his eye.

I have never known DAD like this, nor MUM for that matter, and I can tell that most of the men are very puzzled too. There are still about a dozen or so on 'Golden Explorer', who will continue to talk about Odin and Thor, but they do so quietly and when they think no one is listening. I guess the same goes for the other crews. And sometimes, when I 'happen' to listen in without them knowing, I can hear them talking about that hammer supposedly buried in Hammershus! Little do they know what my friends and I found instead of the hammer. I think one of the first things we must do when we get back is to invite everybody to come and see for themselves that wonderful masterpiece of a sculpture. Just waiting to be admired and, I pray, one day finished? As each of us put a bit of ourselves into it. Oh, how I would love to finish it myself...

Wednesday, July 23rd

"Princess," DAD whispered to me last night just before bedtime. He had not called me that for a very long time. In fact, until we set sail for Norway, he had not spoken to me much at all and had, I remembered, been quite angry with me. "Princess," he repeated, "I know it is dark, but if you look closely, and if you take note of the direction and the sound of the waves, you can tell that we are entering quiet waters. Which means that we are getting ever closer to home. And if you look really hard, you can just about see the outline of Hammershus on the clifftop ahead."

It took me a while to adjust my eyes, but finally, finally, I saw it. This beautiful ruin of a castle, this special place, where some of my greatest treasures had been found, and, I felt, some were hidden still. I couldn't help but touch the cross round my neck. DAD noticed but said nothing, he just walked away, leaving me to enjoy my special moment. Tomorrow, yes, tomorrow morning, we would berth back in the shipyard, to be welcomed home by all our friends.

I went to sleep last night feeling calmer than I had done for a very long time. With all the names of my friends on my heart. Why was it, then, that the very last name on my lips before I closed my eyes was ERLING? What were the chances of me ever seeing him again? And who was he anyway? Or rather, who IS he? More important still, *where* is he? There was no sign of him anywhere when we left Christiania behind.

Saturday, July 26th

We are well and truly back and how good is that! However much we enjoyed Christiania, there is no place like home. Good old Bornholm! And I haven't wasted time, I am the Princess after all.

And so yesterday I called not only all my friends but the whole community together, to speak to them and try and get them to follow me to my secret place, so I could show them all my sculpture! It goes without saying that my nieces and nephews took no persuasion, they were so pleased to see me back safely, and MUM and DAD and the PRIEST were all up for it too. Some of the men, of course, had all kinds of excuses, the main one being the need to get the ships in drydock and repaired, as some of them were still not quite right. And others claimed they had their farming to see to, as not much had been done in their absence. However, in the space of a couple of hours I had more than a hundred people of all ages and beliefs, or none, ready to follow me, and we set a date for next week, Tuesday 29th, with an early start for our pilgrimage. Hoping we could get everything done in a day, now with the longer and warmer summer evenings. I decided that THE PRIEST, MUM and DAD and I would lead the outing, and no one had any objection. My heart was bursting with excitement, and I felt so proud. Soon I would be able to introduce Jesus to so many, who would not have heard about him before, and some who were still on the side of Odin and Thor.

Before I went to bed yesterday, I went and asked THE PRIEST if there was anything I needed to do or prepare before we set out on Tuesday. He told me not to worry. "We'll just go," he said, "sometimes too much preparation can get in the way and leave no room for surprises. And don't forget, not everyone knows what to expect, and some may come along expecting nothing at all. Best not to plan. God will go with us, if not before us, I am sure of it."

And with that I went to bed with not a worry in my little head, just waiting for Tuesday to come.

Sunday, July 27th

I had not expected to write again so quickly, but it was in the church service this morning that THE PRIEST suddenly gave us all an important notice, before starting the sermon. "It has come to my attention," he began, "and I need to share this with you that the Faroe Islands have just appointed their main settlement as their new capital city and named it Torshavn, Thor's Haven. And not only that, Greenland has done the same, nominated a big settlement as their capital city, but they have named theirs Godthaab, meaning Port of Good Hope. So, you see, there is a lot going on with our neighbouring countries, what with Christiania in Norway, from where we have not long returned, Christiania named after Jesus Christ. And it has made me wonder if not we ought to have our own capital city here in Bornholm? May I suggest that when we get to the sculpture on Tuesday, we take some time to think about a name for our capital city?"

There was a deep hush among the congregation, but no one objected, although some did not dare look THE PRIEST in the eyes but looked at the floor instead.

As for me, names for our capital city were already milling about in my head, but I realized that I might not get my own way on this one. Everyone ought to have the chance to choose. I just hoped it would be something with God and Jesus in it, like Christiania. Not something reminding us of Odin or Thor as in the Faroe Islands. Good thing they are so far north, I thought.

Wednesday, July 30th

Now, where do I begin? I just don't know. There is so much going on. And all my nephews and cousins can sense it too, even the youngest ones. There is something in the air that none of us can quite make sense of, not even THE PRIEST nor MUM and DAD.

Let me begin then by saying that when we got to the sculpture, who was there already, sitting patiently, waiting for us. Can you guess?

ERLING, the tall, blue-eyed, blond giant of a Norwegian Viking man, now a Christian, who had been the first to meet us in Christiania, and then not even there when we left. ERLING, the tribesman, so clearly a leader, but I remembered how all his friends had said there was nothing unusual about him coming and going as he wished. And that in fact, although he was not always where they expected or needed him, they felt he was never far away either and always on their minds and in their hearts. Rather like Jesus, I thought.

What I could not understand was how he had found his way from Christiania to Bornholm so soon. Nor how he could have known that we had planned our pilgrimage to the sculpture, so that he could be there waiting for us. Only THE PRIEST seemed to me to know (if his secret smile was anything to go by). But he did not let on. Nor did ERLING say anything, he just quietly welcomed us all.

It was only as we started finding our places to sit by the sculpture that I realized that some recent work had been done to it. It now looked almost complete. Jesus and all his disciples were clearly cut out now, their features individual, from Jesus himself, the only one with a halo, to Simon Peter, the Rock as Jesus called him. And even Judas, the disciple who betrayed Jesus and handed him over to the Romans to die. And who now in the sculpture, next to Jesus at the Communion table, had his eyes downcast towards the floor, unable to face his Master. I had this feeling that perhaps ERLING had been at work, but I had no way of proving it, and I did not want to ask him.

For a long while we just all sat looking and pondering, allowing the sculpture to speak to us. Knowing that some would find this very difficult to take in, while others would probably find their hearts warmed, and maybe for the first time feel their souls stirred as well? I closed my hand round my crucifix, realizing again what a treasure this was to me.

It seemed ages before THE PRIEST finally got up and went to stand next to ERLING. Without any introduction, ERLING now began to speak.

"PRINCESS," he started, "if it were not for you, none of this would have happened. So young, and yet so wise for your years."

I could not believe what I was hearing and could feel a faint blush coming on. Me? Was I really someone special in all this? What about everybody else?

"In every generation," ERLING continued, "I believe God sends someone to guide and inspire us and help us come to believe in Him, and who is to say that you, BRITA, is not one such guiding light? I know, we all know, that it has not always been easy for you to persuade everybody else to believe in Jesus, and there are some who never will. Others may want to, but some think it is all too good to be true, and I can understand where they are coming from too. It *is* sometimes difficult to make sense of everything."

I could tell that ERLING had everybody's attention now, and most of us were waiting for what else was to come. He spoke with such wisdom and authority, and we could not help but listen.

"Well, we are here by the sculpture now, the sculpture that BRITA found. But you will see that although it looks very different and much better now than it did in the early days, there are still a few bits and pieces missing. Most of the disciples have their eyes clearly focused on Jesus, but there are one or two where the eyes seem to be not yet quite finished. And have you noticed that some of the disciples do not seem to have a heart beating for their Lord?"

And this is when I noticed, and no doubt many others, that indeed each of the characters in the sculpture had a visible heart, Jesus's of course the biggest of all, but some of the hearts seemed only half drawn, not yet complete.

"Those hearts," said ERLING, "may never look different in the sculpture, but if each of you decide that you want a heart for Jesus, then believe me, you will feel a difference in your lives, a big difference."

I could tell that ERLING was coming to the end of his talk for now, but I also sensed that there was one more important message to come. When, finally, it did come, it took not only me, but many of the others, by surprise and made us feel rather uneasy.

"Even as we are gathered here," said ERLING, "there are longboats on the way to Bornholm from as far away as Greenland and the Faroe Islands. A very long journey, sure, but some of the boats are modern and fast, and I believe they will begin to arrive here in a month's time, by early September for sure. And that is when a big sea battle will take place, between the Thor worshippers from the Faroe Islands on one hand, and the Jesus believers from Greenland on the other. Meeting us here on our island, where more and more are turning to Jesus, but where we still have many also who prefer to believe in Odin and Thor. So, what will happen, who can tell? However, the good news is that our friends from Christiania are also preparing to come and are getting ready for battle, and we all know whose side they are on, don't we?"

I was disturbed at hearing this and asked ERLING if he thought blood would be spilled and people killed? "Almost certainly," he said, "and on both sides too. We just need to be sure that we are on the right side, don't we? And don't forget, although the boats from the Faroe Islands are modern and fast, they come from a very small country. I dare say they will find it hard work to battle and win against those on the way from Norway and Greenland, not to mention you Danes here in Bornholm."

It took a long while before anything else happened, and perhaps some of us were preparing to get ready for returning home, when THE PRIEST moved forward and said, "We must not forget that there is another reason why we are here today. We must choose a name for our new capital. I want all of you to have the opportunity to think of one, and whichever ends up with the most votes is the winner. I wonder if I can ask ERLING to announce the result. As soon as you have a name, let ERLING know, so he can make a note of it. And we will wait for the result before we return home."

We all nodded and started thinking. Not everybody had any idea what to suggest, but in the end thirty suggestions had been presented to ERLING. And it was with great anticipation and excitement we heard him announce the result.

"Not surprisingly," he began, "there are some among us here who are still not sure where we stand on this, and some who still favour Odin and Thor. So, it is understandable that we have both Odin's Haven and Thor's Bay as suggestions, in fact two votes for each. This leaves twenty-six proposals, and they all point to God or Jesus. The clear winner with fifteen votes is GUDHJEM ("God's Dwelling"). Thank you all for your contributions. Let us head home and soon we will have an official naming ceremony and a party and start getting the city – Gudhjem - ready for battle. To receive friends and enemies alike. Do not worry, all will be well. Even if I may not be here with you in person all the time, I have every faith in you. Perhaps I will be needed elsewhere soon, but you have BRITA, and you have MUM and DAD, and you have THE PRIEST, and you will soon have your friends from Greenland and Norway to lead you and see you to victory."

Our walk home took place almost in total silence. I cannot remember ever seeing over a hundred people make so little noise.

Thursday, August 1st

My friends and I are exhausted today and have spent much time simply playing and relaxing, without thinking too hard and for too long. We all feel these are uncertain times, and if we are honest, we are a bit scared, but also just a bit excited. About all these foreigners coming soon, and what might happen when they do. A big sea battle, ERLING had said, and some lives will be lost. On both sides. Never a pleasant thought but being the Princess I could not be seen to bury my head in the sand. I had to be strong for everybody.

Saturday, August 3rd

Yesterday, out of curiosity, I asked MUM and DAD how, with all this going on, no one had mentioned Sweden? I knew there were Vikings in that country too, and after all, Bornholm sits at the bottom of Sweden, although we belong to Denmark, but ERLING had not mentioned our neighbours at all. And it puzzled me.

"Well, you see, Princess," DAD started, "Sweden has always tried to keep out of conflict, they have always wanted to stay neutral, when other countries threatened to go to war. And I guess this is what is happening again now. I don't really know, but that's my guess. I wouldn't worry about it, what will be will be, and we have God on our side, don't we?"

Not for the first time I could hardly believe what had happened to DAD. How he had changed. And in such a short time too. Always an Odin and Thor man, until he met those Norwegians at Christiania and saw and felt their welcome and absolute faith and certainty that all would be well with the world.

I was so pleased and squeezed his hand, while holding on to my crucifix with the other.

Monday, August 5th

During the church service yesterday, and I am sorry to say while THE PRIEST delivered his sermon, it suddenly came to me that perhaps I ought to let my friends write a little bit in my Journal. Or at least tell me what they would like me to write about how they look at everything that is happening. After all, soon enough Bornholm will be visited, or invaded, by many foreigners, some friendly, others not, and it might be good for all of us to know where we stand and what we think, if anything. So, after Sunday lunch I called them all together, including little SKOLL, born so recently, since I started my Journal in fact, and only a few months old. I don't expect him to have a lot to say just yet! But his time will come!

They all thought it was a great idea and suggested I start with the oldest first and finish with the youngest – SKOLL. They also felt it was best to let me do the writing, and they would take it in turns to meet with me, one to one, and dictate what they would like me to write. Without interruption from me, without any questions being asked. I look quite forward to this, and it will help us kill time during this long, lazy summer month, while we wait for September. We decided to start the exercise on Wednesday and then break for a couple of days, before the next one came to see me.

Wednesday, August 7th – YULLA'S STORY

Yes, I am the oldest in our group, and I think it is rather sweet and very respectful of BRITA to let me start our stories. I know she is very fond of writing her Journal, and these are certainly interesting times with lots to write about, and it seems with the best still to come? I have to say I am not totally convinced about all this Jesus business, but I am not denying it either, and when occasionally I do go to church, I admit there is a lot of love and kindness being spoken by THE PRIEST.

However, when we first went to Hammershus to look for Thor's hammer, I was *very* disappointed when we did not find it. Why name a fortress Hammershus, if there is not even a hammer to be found? Ridiculous if you ask me. And when instead of the hammer all these other symbols started appearing, which had nothing to do with Odin and Thor, I felt cheated, I felt angry, and maybe, if I am being honest, I feel a bit like that still.

Am I frightened about the next few weeks and perhaps months to come? Do I fear the sea battle which ERLING believes will have to happen? Am I unsure about the outcome? Definitely. Do I look forward to all those Norwegian Vikings coming to our shores? Without a doubt! All these gorgeous men, although when INGRID and I first went to Christiania there was no catch, sadly. I really want to find a tall, handsome seafaring Viking man, and if not among the Norwegians, perhaps one of the Faroe Island warriors will do nicely? Even if he believes in Odin and Thor rather than Jesus. We wait and see.

Meanwhile, I will let BRITA continue doing what she does best. Anyone who can convert even DAD and turn him away from Odin and Thor must be worth their salt, but no, I am not at all sure yet, and that is being honest.

Saturday, August 10th – INGRID'S STORY

To be honest, I have my hands full most of the time keeping an eye on BJORN, bless him, who, until SKOLL was born, was the youngest of us all. I shall never forget our first trip to Hammershus, when he kept shouting, "Wait for me, wait for me!" and of course we did, waited for him to catch up, him being so little and innocent.

YULLA and I are finding most of what is going on very puzzling and confusing. I am not sure what or whom I believe in anymore, although I have to say that whenever THE PRIEST talks about Jesus, there always seems to be so much commitment required to follow him and believe in him. It is not like Odin and Thor, who in the main seem to leave us well alone, up there somewhere in their heavens. Jesus, on the other hand, sometimes seems far too near, although we cannot see him or touch him. A bit like this fellow ERLING. I can't make sense of him either. But boy, is he good looking! I bet he's taken already by some beautiful Norwegian woman, though. YULLA and I can only hope that someone among the Greenlanders, perhaps, may find us attractive, or vice versa? When they come…

I just don't know what to make of things at present, however hard I try. Fortunately, I do not feel scared or uncertain about the future, I rather sense a kind of peace, which I am not sure where comes from. A kind of certainty that everything will be okay. Maybe not all at once, but in time.

I do miss our trips to Hammershus, when we went hunting for that hammer! Not that I was really bothered one way or the other, whether it was there or not, but the excitement of looking was great. If there is time before all the ships start arriving, I would like another expedition, but I guess BRITA has other and more important things on her mind right now.

Tuesday, August 13th – AIFE'S STORY

I cannot wait for all these foreigners to arrive, and I quite relish the thought of a good battle myself. Things can get rather boring when there is not much going on. I think RUNE feels the same, although he is so quiet you cannot always tell.

As for me, I do a lot of exercising and keeping fit, and I think I can punch the daylight out of the best of them! We'll see. Perhaps I shouldn't be so violent in my thinking, but I guess they must have known when they named me. Great Warrior Woman is what my name means, and a Great Warrior is what I aim to be.

Like most of my friends, I am not sure about Jesus. Nor about Odin and Thor for that matter. None of them really make that much difference to me, I don't feel. I'm happy as I am without all this supernatural talk going on, and I honestly can't remember when I last attended a Sunday service. Although, on the few occasions I have, I do remember a certain kind of peace, of feeling loved and respected, but I cannot accept that such feelings are reserved for an hour or so on a Sunday. I cannot fathom what BRITA is making of everything, but I must admit she seems happier and busier than I have ever known her. And she's a good leader with many ideas. We are fortunate to have her.

Thursday, August 15th – RUNE'S STORY

Yes, they call me the quiet one, the mysterious one, which of course is what my name means. But I don't mind that, in fact I think that is quite alright, for this allows me to think or say or do what I like, and no one will batter an eyelid.

I am finding it very difficult to make sense of most of what is happening in all our lives. There seems to be no rhyme or reason to it if you ask me. Alright, I know BRITA is always busy trying to write everything down in her diary, as and when it happens, but whenever we ask if we may have a look at her notes, she always says, "No, what I write is between Jesus and myself."

Jesus? Probably the greatest mystery of all, and I thought Odin and Thor were hard enough to come to terms with. Not that I really tried that hard, ever. But Jesus? And this man ERLING, now he really puzzles me. Here one moment, gone the next, but he seems to know about everything going on and about what is going to happen as well. Uncanny.

The biggest change I have seen lately is in DAD. He seems a completely different man now. Always the leader of the colony, the commander of the longboats, all the longboats, the one whom everybody bowed to and obeyed. And a true believer in Odin and Thor. But now? I'm not sure, and I am not sure he is sure either (if that makes any sense?).

I guess all I can do for now is go with the flow and see what happens.

Saturday, August 17th – FRIDA'S STORY

I think it is very kind of BRITA to hand over to me now, without wanting to write anything for herself, as she is next in line. As she says, I write my journal notes anyway, it's YOUR turn now, all of you, I just want to learn and listen and find out where you are all coming from.

For someone as young as I am, it is very hard to express what I feel and what I think. Most of the time I just go along happily with all the others, with no real opinion of my own, or that is how it feels.

Having said that, I did enjoy it when we all met with ERLING and the PRIEST at Hammershus, and we were told about all these seafarers about to arrive from so many different countries. Some friendly, others not so. Even the talk about some fierce battles about to happen does not really scare me. I feel quite at peace here on this lovely island, and I trust my friends, and BRITA especially, to keep us all safe. She is indeed our little Princess, and I love her to bits.

There is not much more I can say here and now. LEIF is next, and I guess he will be even briefer than me, as he is so much younger, and then LOVA and BJORN, bless them. As for SKOLL, I guess he will just smile sweetly and wonder where the next drop of milk and cuddle may come from? He is so young, but adorable, and as BRITA says sometimes, he is the one for whom we must all continue to pray to Jesus to make this place even safer and better to live in. Never mind how long it takes or what obstacles may get in the way. He is the next generation.

I cannot say I fully understand how she can trust Jesus to help us, but nor can I say that I do not believe her.

Tuesday, August 20ᵗʰ – LEIF, LOVA, BJORN AND SKOLL

When FRIDA returned from her meeting with BRITA, the two of them had discussed that it might be better if the rest of us, being the youngest by far, went together and asked BRITA to interview us as a group. So, I, LEIF, being the oldest of the youngest, agreed to represent us all as best I could. The meeting went something like this:

BRITA: I have really enjoyed listening to so many of you over the last couple of weeks, and now we come to the four of you. Being so young, compared to the others, is there anything you are looking forward to or perhaps a bit frightened about, when you think of the next few weeks ahead?

LEIF: We cannot wait to see all the ships arriving from so many different countries, near and far. What a sight that will be. We just hope they will not all come at once, as where would we put them? The harbour is not big enough! We also quite look forward to a good, old sea battle, as we are too young to remember the last one, and we just hope we will win and that not too many lives will be lost.

BRITA: Yes, let's hope Jesus will look after us. What do the four of you make of Jesus?

LEIF: Well, I don't think BJORN and SKOLL are too bothered, they are far too young to understand. As for LOVA and me, we are not sure. There is so much about him we just do not understand, especially when THE PRIEST goes on for too long in his sermons. We get lost, and we think sometimes he gets himself lost too. What do *you* think, BRITA.

BRITA: I love Jesus with all my heart, with all my mind, and with all my soul. And why? Because of what I have seen him do to DAD, who only ever believed in Odin and Thor. But look where that has got him, or any of us for that matter. I would rather believe in someone, who talks about love and care and not being frightened but brave and hopeful. That is why I enjoy listening to THE PRIEST, even when he does get a big long-winded, as you say. He means well.

LEIF: And what about this ERLING? Who is he, BRITA? On one hand he is almost like one of us, while on the other hand he just seems to come and go as he pleases, leaving so much for us little people to do for ourselves. Who is he, BRITA? Is he a good man like Jesus, or is he a hero of some kind to the people of Norway? Where did he first come from, and where do you think he will be going next. And to whom?

BRITA: You are asking some wonderful questions, LEIF. Good for you. Keep asking questions, I do, for that is the best way to find answers, in God's time. Maybe not immediately, but before you know it, things will become clear to all of us. I am sure of it. But first it looks like we must go through some troubled times?

LEIF: You have not answered my questions. We want to know who this ERLING is.

BRITA: Well, the best I can say is that he reminds me a bit about a follower of Jesus called PAUL, who travelled the world, by ship, by horse and on foot. And he spread the word and told everybody he met about Jesus, about God. He never tired of doing that. And because the world is so big, and there were so many people to see, PAUL could not always stay in one place very long. Just like ERLING, he had to move on. But he never moved on, until he had found someone to keep sharing the good news about Jesus. And I think that is what ERLING is doing here and now for us. Using us, all ten of us young people, to do and share something wonderful. Even little SKOLL, who cannot speak properly yet, will one day have something to say about Jesus. I am sure of it.

LEIF: Thank you, BRITA. I think you have answered all our questions now.

BRITA: And thank you, LEIF. I am so glad we have had this interview, and I can tell all four of you have done a lot of thinking. Now, let us get ready for whatever is to happen, and soon. It cannot be long before the first boats start arriving. Will they be friend or enemy, I wonder? Let battle commence!

Friday, August 23rd

I cannot believe I finished my last sentence with 'Let battle commence' – for if I had known then what I know now, I would probably have chosen something else to say, or better still, kept quiet.

Ships are indeed arriving on the horizon, and so many of them too. Judging from the colours and shapes of their sails and the writings on them, they are the ones coming from Iceland, so enemy ones, remembering that the capital city of Iceland is Thorshavn, Thor's Haven. Meaning that the Icelanders are not followers of Jesus at all, but of Odin and Thor. All I, all *we* can hope for now is that ships from Greenland and Norway will start arriving too, as otherwise there could be big trouble ahead.

DAD has been spending a lot of time with THE PRIEST in prayer, I have noticed, and I too spend as much time as I can on my own at the sculpture. Sometimes just quietly, sometimes praying out loud. Both THE PRIEST and ERLING have told me often that Jesus too spent a lot of time praying to God, his Father, when things got difficult. I do think early next week I will invite all my friends to join me up here in prayer. And in any case, being set on a cliff, Hammershus is also the best place for us to see how the ships are progressing. For the moment they seem to be in no great hurry, moving very slowly, with a long way still to go before they reach our shores.

Monday, August 26th

Yesterday was the first church service I can remember with the building filled to bursting point. There was standing room only, and it seemed as if the whole population of Bornholm had come to hear words of hope and comfort from THE PRIEST. And they were not disappointed. He spoke well and honestly and lovingly and told us all not to worry but remain brave and hopeful. The only disappointment to many was that ERLING was not there. Many had come to meet him and express their respect for him, and now, when he was most needed, it seemed he had once again travelled on somewhere else. Suddenly and secretly, almost as if he had never been here in the first place. But I knew this wasn't true. I knew in my heart that ERLING was never far away and that he would always remember and stay loyal to this small island of ours. I was convinced we had not heard or seen the last of him. But it was no good saying anything. People were fearful and found it hard to believe in good news right now.

After the service, DAD took a dozen of his men down to the harbour and the docks to check our ships, to make sure that they were ready for battle at a moment's notice, especially if help did not arrive from Greenland or Norway in time.

Sunday, September 1st

A whole week almost gone and not a note in my journal. Not surprising perhaps with nothing much to report. Except for ships continuing to approach our island, but most of them too far away for us to say where they were coming from. And again, we had to ask the question, "Are they friend or foe?"

Once again, what seemed like most of the population got together to hear what THE PRIEST might have to say by way of comfort and assurance. But I know that what most of them really came for was in the hope of finding ERLING and see that he had returned to us. Yet again we were disappointed.

I agreed with my friends that it was high time to return to Hammershus, to the highest point of the castle, so that we could see for ourselves what was going on. And we agreed to meet in secret tomorrow, as we wanted no one else to know or think they could join us. This was going to be *our* private expedition, no one else's.

And so, with YULLA , INGRID, AIFE, RUNE, FRIDA, LEIF, LOVA, BORN and even little SKOLL onboard and ready for adventure, I , BRITA, took charge yet again, as we began to march towards the high cliffs of Hammershus. Not knowing what to expect or what we might see out there on the high seas...

Tuesday, September 3rd

Our first port of call at Hammershus was the sculpture, my spiritual home as I had come to see it, and I asked them all to join me in prayer. Not everyone did. I knew from the interviews earlier that I could never expect that. But those who didn't still respected those who did, by just withdrawing slightly and letting us get on with it.

We then continued to the highest point of the island, and what we saw took our breaths away.

The ships from Iceland seemed very close now, and we could tell them from the colours of their flags, but other longboats, with the colours of Norway and Greenland, were not far behind and getting closer at quite some speed. We sensed that there were far more of those, and that they moved faster than the Icelanders. Soon, we feared, they would catch up, and no doubt there would be a ferocious sea battle starting. Unless...

I don't know what made me do so, but I turned my head to look down at our docks, where again there was much activity. Our own ships were getting ready to go out and meet the invaders, or visitors, we were not yet sure what we should call them. Or who might be coming as friends rather than enemies.

It was as I turned back to look out over the sea that I heard YULLA shriek and point towards the site of the sculpture we had just left. And there he was, ERLING. The wanderer had returned, and there and then I felt in my heart that everything would be okay.

Rather than coming to join us, ERLING did as if he had not even noticed us. Instead, he went to a different lookout point from ours, where quietly he fell on his knees in deep prayer and stayed like that for what seemed a very long time.

Suddenly we heard the first shots being fired from the cannons on the Icelandic boats towards the fleet approaching them fast. And we knew then that battle had commenced, especially when we looked back into the docks and saw DAD's longboats begin to depart and join in the "fun".

As a group, we decided to retreat to relative safety. I felt a little sad leaving ERLING behind. He was still deep in prayer some distance away from us, but again I felt a real sense of peace, and a belief that although it might not look like it right now, everything would be okay. ERLING was here.

Thursday, September 5th

Yesterday saw some of the fiercest battles I can remember in my young life, as the boats from Norway and Greenland came ever nearer and fired their cannons at the Icelanders. Many of the shots missed and landed in the sea, but some hit the decks, and fires could be seen on some of the boats, as their crews plunged into the water to escape injury and possible death. There is no question that the Icelandic Vikings are outnumbered about 10 to 1, but even so, they put up a good fight. Some stayed on deck to see their battles through, as the enemy drew alongside and clambered onboard with their swords and axes at the ready.

To start with, it seemed there was no need for DAD and his fleet to join in anything, but we could clearly see that they were battle ready and prepared for combat at any time. There was no way they were going to stay in the docks for longer than necessary and risk becoming captured there, with nowhere to go. However, for the moment, they could take a breather and simply watch proceedings.

Saturday, September 7th

Yesterday saw the first wounded Icelanders arrive in small boats to the shore. From here they were transported to the hastily prepared infirmary at Hammershus, to be cared for and restored to good health. We islanders had decided long ago that friend or foe would be treated the same and with respect and not be left to die from their wounds, and certainly never alone. MUM and many volunteers from the farms on the island took it in turns to provide the necessary bandages and medical equipment. And so, miraculously, in the first few days, and although many were badly wounded, we had no casualties. No one died.

Sunday, September 8th

They say Sunday is a day of rest, but you could fool me! The battles are just as ferocious today, if not more so, and DAD and his men have now left port to join forces with the

Norwegians and Greenlanders. If it carries on like this, it surely cannot be long before the Icelanders are totally humiliated and forced to lay down their weapons. But they are a stubborn lot. Their cries and petitions of seeking help from Odin and Thor are relentless, and my friends and I truly wonder how it is all going to end. Well, we *know* it will end in victory for us, but how long will it take before the first casualties are brough to shore. How many good men will have to perish?

And just as we were thinking these things and watching the drama playing out at sea; just as we really began to fear that much blood would be shed, and not only among the Icelanders; right at this precise moment did we see ERLING at the highest point of the island, standing up tall and waving his arms in the air for everyone to see. For a moment the battle noise seemed to cease, as all the warriors waited to hear and see what would happen next. And they were not disappointed.

Without even raising his voice very much, knowing that water carries sound perfectly, and knowing that he had everyone's attention, he began with words that will stay with me forever.

"Friends, what on earth are we playing at? Why are we at each other's throats? What are we hoping to achieve? Already many good men have been badly wounded, and many ships are damaged by fire, some perhaps beyond repair. How much more fear and agony do we want to face? Have we not had enough already?"

No one said anything, but despite the wind and the roaring of the sea, it was as if you could hear a pin drop.

"Jesus," he continued, "the One I believe in always used to say that if an army with, say, ten thousand men go towards another army with twenty thousand, does it not make sense for the smaller army to send out someone to try and negotiate with the commander of the bigger army?"

Again, he waited as if to see if anyone was going to argue or let battle recommence, but neither happened. The warriors, whatever nationality, wherever they came from, wanted to hear more from this giant of a man. Who spoke with such authority and warmth.

"Jesus also said love your enemy as you love yourself. Now, I cannot know how many of you love yourselves, but I guess not very many. It is a very difficult thing to do, for we all do or say silly things again and again. And if you are like me, we feel so awful afterwards. But Jesus said, "Even if you do something stupid at times, but then regret it and ask God for forgiveness, and mean it and are serious about it, then God will forgive you and give you a chance to start afresh. Just think about that."

With this, ERLING prepared to take his leave, having evidently said all he wanted to say on this occasion. And like so many times before, when we next looked at the hilltop, he was no longer there. Only his words seemed to linger in the air for quite some time...

When battle did start again, it was without much of the ferocity and anger with which it had all begun. There seemed to be no real soul or desire in it. I began to think that maybe, just maybe, things were about to change? And especially so when I saw DAD commandeer his fleet to return to the docks without a single shot having been fired from any of his ships. Unheard of!

Tuesday, September 10th

Today, barely a week since it all started, the sea is calm. The Icelandic fleet, now down to just four operational ships, is securely anchored in the docks, the battle has finished. The Greenlanders and the Norwegians have started their return journeys, perhaps feeling that they have secured a great victory, perhaps not? Everything went rather tame and quiet after ERLING's big speech. No one really seemed to feel they had won or lost. All we are left with on the island are the Icelandic Vikings at the infirmary, being well tended to, fed and watered. About thirty of them. Another fifty or so have been welcomed to the homes of the islanders, for as long as it takes. And many have offered to work on the farms and to help with the building of our new capital, Gudhjem, God's Dwelling. How long they will stay, who can tell, but I guess they will wait until all their wounds are healed and then return home on their four remaining ships. We wait and see. DAD says they are welcome to stay for as long as they like.

Friday, September 13th

Lucky for some! Reports are coming in that unlike us on this wonderful island of ours, Vikings in many other countries are still planning some long and wonderful voyages, or so they say. They want to go as far afield as possible and see if they can conquer nations they have not even thought about so far. England and Normandy are among them, but they are also talking about going to the far east. I cannot believe it, but MUM and DAD are not showing any interest at all in joining them. Not so long ago they would have been first in the queue for sure, but not now. So much has changed in what seems a very short time, and our island is becoming an even happier place than it was before. Maybe it is because we are so far away from the mainland and the heat of the action, I don't know, but I don't mind. I like the peace and quiet.

Sunday, September 15th

Other reports are coming in now that in some countries, and some not too far away from us, the Viking way of life seems to be coming to a halt or being taken over by something else. Some people are even whispering that perhaps we have had our time, and that something new is just about to happen. One part of me feels I should be upset at hearing this – after all, I love being the Viking Princess – but then another part seems to say that nothing and no one last forever, and that we should just try to make the best of every new day, while we can. I can tell that my friends are as puzzled as I am, and many of the adults too, but we just get on with our daily work, and the church is full to bursting now every Sunday. They are even talking about building a second and bigger one soon. This is unheard of. And even more surprisingly, no one ever talks about Thor's hammer anymore and where or how to find it! It is almost as if it does not matter any longer.

No one has seen or heard from ERLING since his speech that changed everything for so many and put a stop to the sea battle. Perhaps he is somewhere else entirely now? YULLA and INGRID admitted to me only yesterday that they were both beginning to take a fancy to him. One of them is bad enough! Poor ERLING that's all I can say… I hope he can run faster than they can!

Wednesday, September 18th

YULLA and INGRID summoned us all to what they called an emergency meeting near the infirmary at Hammershus yesterday. Highly unusual, as it is normally me, the Princess, who calls the meetings on this island. However, I could tell it was urgent, so we all trooped up to hear what they had to say, even the two youngest, BJORN and SKOL. However, we agreed to go and see how the poor Icelanders were getting on in the infirmary first. We were pleased to discover that most of them had recovered well and would soon be able to join their friends already helping on our farms. Not only that but many of them were also keen to help build the second church. They even suggested that we could pull down the pagan temple used for worshipping Odin and Thor, and then use some of that material to build the church, where we could worship Jesus instead. Music to my ears!

We also made a detour to the sculpture, and perhaps it was my imagination, but I have never seen Jesus and his disciples look so radiant. It was almost as if they too were feeling our sense of love and respect for Christianity. As if they were coming alive, although of course they were but stone and mortar. I held on to my cross, my treasured necklace, and thanked God for what He continued to do.

Anyway, YULLA and INGRID had managed to trace ERLING yesterday and declared their love for him. They sobbed deeply as they shared with us all that while ERLING felt honoured by the interest in him shown by two such beautiful young ladies, he was sorry to say he could not and would not commit himself. He was far too busy trying to spread the Word, and in fact in just a few days' time he intended to travel all the way to America, to see what he might do to spread the name of Jesus there. He imagined he would be away for several months.

No wonder YULLA and INGRID were not best pleased, but good for ERLING that he felt he had more important work to do. And after all, he could leave Bornholm safely in the knowledge that everything was fine here, with more and more people every day coming to know Jesus.

My heart was beating with sympathy for the girls, of course, but above all with love for everything ERLING and the PRIESTS had helped me believe in. Until I heard BJORN ask, "While we are all here, can we not have one more go at finding Thor's hammer?"

I did not know where to put myself, but fortunately AIFE and RUNE had the good sense to suggest that as it was getting late, perhaps best leave that for another day, and soon? They all agreed, except me who had nothing to say on the matter. Nothing at all.

Wednesday, September 25th

A whole week gone. And so has ERLING. I do not expect to see him again in a hurry. He seemed to know where this land of America might be, but the rest of us were none the wiser. Least of all DAD, who was never known for his sense of direction at the best of times.

BJORN went on and on about going back to Hammershus and look for that hammer, and in the end, I took pity on him. He and I, joined by AIFE and RUNE returned to the parts of the castle we had already investigated earlier in the year. The others stayed behind, whether they thought it was a waste of time, or just did not care, I do not know.

We found nothing. And I don't think we ever shall.

In this last week the building of the second church has really gathered speed. The pagan temple has been taken apart, and the two PRIESTS are arguing about who will be looking after which church. MUM and DAD try not to get involved in that side of things, and most of the islanders are happy just knowing that soon there will be two places for them to choose between and go to on a Sunday.

During the early part of this week the infirmary finally released the last of the wounded Icelanders. None of them are talking about going back to Iceland. All of them keep saying what a lovely island Bornholm is, and what a great atmosphere of love and concern for each other we have.

However, it is not like this everywhere. We keep getting reports in from other parts of the world that the Viking population is struggling. At the same time, it seems that those of us who believe in Jesus are finding an inner peace and calm even in the most difficult of circumstances. Even my friends are beginning to say the same. We are a happy bunch.

The biggest worry, says DAD, is the talk about an invasion of England and Normandy, which seems to take up a lot of preparation in many countries. And he wonders how long it may be before the Bornholm Vikings are asked to join.

I cannot help looking back at how DAD used to be, and how he is now. When the year started, he would have dropped everything for a good, long fight, but not so now. It is almost as if he wants the quiet life to last forever.

Friday, September 27th

Autumn is at its highest now and the weather remains mild, but the days are getting shorter, and we know that soon winter will set in. If past winters are anything to go by, all too soon the seas will freeze over, and the temperatures drop, and the bleak and cold winter nights may then continue for five months or more. Yes, we should be used to it, but still, it comes as a surprise every year. Many on the island reckon that we have perhaps another three weeks, until the middle of October, to finish the second church and the completion of our capital Gudhjem. We are all getting very busy and helping out wherever we can.

The church is filled to the rafters every Sunday, and many who used to worship Thor and Odin in the pagan temple are coming to us now. They say it's because they have nowhere else to go, but I don't believe that. I reckon Jesus is making himself known to them, whether they like it or not. And maybe through something we say or do, those of us who already trust in him?

Monday, September 30th

After church yesterday, I went on my own to sit by the sculpture, among Jesus and the disciples. And again, it was as if there were a new 'glow' coming over them, simply by someone like me coming close and spending time with them. For the first time ever, I even ventured right up to Jesus and squeezed in by his side, between him and Simon Peter, the disciple he loved the most. I remembered someone saying that it is as we get ever closer to him that he becomes the most real to us. And that for some it may take longer than for others. I also remembered how all of the PRIESTS, at some point or another, had said or written to me that God had plans for me, and that I would be an inspiration to many on the island.

I drew closer to Jesus, looked at Simon Peter, and it was almost as if I could see a twinkle in his eyes.

I spent more than an hour in that holy and wonderful place, just me and my friends. And when I got home, I told MUM and DAD all about it. Realizing that not so very long ago, DAD would either have laughed his head off or screamed at me, but not now. This time he held me in a long and warm embrace, and with tears streaming down his face said these wonderful words, "If it were not for you, Princess, where would we be? Where would I be for a start? I have never been happier that when I came to know Jesus, and I wonder if I ever would have known him without you?"

I did not know what to say, so I just stayed quiet and relished the moment, embraced by DAD, and surrounded by the love of God.

Wednesday, October 2nd

I can hardly believe it, it is only a week since ERLING set off for foreign shores, and already I have received a letter from him. Not YULLA and not INGRID, but little me, the Princess. I feel very honoured. I will wait until the chores are done and then have a look and a read quietly tonight. All is going well with the new church building as you can imagine, with over a hundred people working on it, and MUM trying to keep up with all the food required. Building a church is hungry work!

....

And so, it's quiet, and I'm on my own, and it is time to read ERLING'S letter.

"Dear BRITA, I am only a few days and nights into my very long voyage, but all is going well, the oarsmen are working hard, and God is with us every step. I am so grateful to DAD that he could spare me one of his longboats and the men to push it along.

You may wonder why I am writing to you and not to YULLA or INGRID, although I have no problem with you sharing this letter with them if you wish. It is just that you have always been my soulmate, ever since I first set eyes on you. And it has nothing to do with me finding you attractive – although you are – but everything to do with your love for and trust in Jesus. I think you will go far, BRITA, and one day become a true inspiration for so many people. Perhaps you already are? Don't worry if not everybody will come to understand your way of thinking all at once, that never happens. Just keep going and never give up. Visit your sculpture again and again. And one day you should invite MUM and DAD, just the two of them, to join you. I mean it. They have already come so far, but you can help them come closer still to Jesus.

I cannot say when I will be back on the island. I cannot even say **whether** I'll be back. Perhaps. Perhaps not. It depends on the reception we get in America. They may be friendly, but then again, they may be anything but. I need to be prepared for anything, and I am.

I do hope to be back for Christmas, though. Yes, Christmas, BRITA. The day when we celebrate the birth of Jesus. Just like at Easter time we remember his death and crucifixion, and his coming back to life again. But you haven't celebrated Easter yet on the island, BRITA, perhaps next year, it is early days. But Christmas you will, and you will love it.

I want you to prepare the islanders for Christmas. Tell them that this will be all about the birth of Jesus. About having a party, a real feast, being happy and thankful, seeing the churches packed with people, and of course lots and lots of prayer. Will you promise me, BRITA, that you will start now preparing everyone for Christmas? You have until nearly the end of December, which is when we celebrate Christmas. But the time is coming when winter sets in, and there won't be anything much else you or anyone can do, with the shorter days and longer nights. In my next letter, hopefully in a week's time, I will tell you how to go about it all, but NOW is the time to start thinking about it. How you do that I leave with you. You will find a way.

All my love

ERLING

I read the letter again, I think and pray about it, and soon decide that in the next few days I will share it with MUM and DAD and all my friends in a special meeting. And yes, perhaps with the two PRIESTS as well. No, with the two PRIESTS for sure. For I have a feeling that the two churches will be filled to breaking point at Christmas time, so the PRIESTS will be busier than ever.

I cannot wait for ERLING'S next letter with all the details, but nor can I wait until then to call my meeting. I must act now.

Saturday, October 5th

We met yesterday by the sculpture, where else? MUM and DAD, the two PRIESTS, and then YULLA and INGRID, AIFE, RUNE, FRIDA, LEIF, LOVA, BJORN and even little SKOL, the youngest among us. I, BRITA, the Princess, opened the meeting with a prayer and then I read ERLING'S letter. I could tell that YULLA and INGRID were sad, when it seemed that ERLING preferred me to them, but they soon calmed down and listened intently as I continued with the rest of the letter.

The PRIESTS smiled happily, and I realized that of course they would know everything about Christmas and how to celebrate it. I also sensed that they were not going to take over but were as interested as the rest of us in waiting for ERLING'S next letter. MUM and DAD looked happy too but also just a little puzzled. MUM was probably wondering how to cope with all that extra food that seemed to be involved. AIFE and RUNE, who were still not quite sure about all this Jesus thing, said they would look forward to a great big party. FRIDA and LEIF were not too worried one way or the other but would happily go along with everybody else. Which left LOVA, BJORN and SKOL, who of course were the youngest and with not a lot to contribute. BJORN was still moaning about not finding Thor's hammer.

There weren't any real questions, those of us with any views simply agreed that yes, Christmas seemed like a great idea, and that we would meet again when the next letter arrived from ERLING. I would let them know. And then we could really start planning.

Before we left, INGRID stood up and said, with tears in her eyes, "Best of all, ERLING is hoping to be back with us for Christmas, isn't he, BRITA? He says so in his letter."

I could only agree, but somewhere in my heart I felt a burning pain. I did not share that with anyone, but after they had left, I stayed behind at the sculpture, in prayer. I could not get rid of the feeling that not everything might go to plan, and a part of me even wondered if we would see ERLING again? Ever.

Wednesday, October 9th

This is such a happy day on the island. The second church stands ready and will be receiving its first worshippers on Sunday. Each of our two churches can hold up to 300 people, and the PRIESTS are confident that they will get them. They are even talking about standing room only. I wish…

Also, this morning, ERLING'S second letter arrived. I have not opened it yet but have decided to wait until after the church service on Sunday morning. And then maybe tell all the islanders from the pulpit that something very special will happen come Christmas, and that I now have all the instructions from ERLING. It is going to be hard to wait with the letter until then, but all good things are worth waiting for. Of course, I can only be in one church, but I am sure the word will soon spread to the second one too.

Monday, October 14th

Sunday went very well. The PRIEST from Malta, who took the service in the church I was in, allowed me to share ERLING'S letter with the congregation. And he also promised to keep the PRIEST from Egypt (in the other church) fully informed later in the day, so that he could inform *his* congregation too. All good!

This is what ERLING wrote, and what therefore I shared with everybody. However, I include my own thoughts on some of the things he wrote, wondering how on earth he could have known. I did not share any of that with anyone, though.

Dear BRITA and all my friends on the island of Bornholm,

I guess by now those who were wounded in the sea battle will have recovered and be fully occupied with work on the island, so my greetings go to those too.

(Now, how could ERLING know that this is precisely what is happening? Is he psychic or something?)

Last time I wrote to BRITA, I promised her that my next, and perhaps final, letter would include details about a very big and wonderful celebration I want you to think about this year. It is called Christmas, and it marks the birth of our Lord and Saviour Jesus. You may wonder why this late in the year, and do we really know in what month or what year he was born? The answer is no, not for certain, but many people throughout the world have agreed that December is a good month to celebrate. A bit of light in all the darkness of winter. I hope you are with me this far.

(Of course, ERLING, I thought, you are as clear as mud, but we all love you…)

I know very well, ERLING continued, that you all have your little birthdays every year on certain days, and that you all celebrate them with your friends and families, and that is great. However, the birthday I am talking about is for the greatest man who ever lived, and not just a man, but the Son of God Himself. And you don't get bigger than that.

(Now you are talking, ERLING, but please, can you get on with it, the people here don't want another sermon).

So, here is what I want you to do so you can start preparing now to mark the birth of Jesus, almost one thousand years ago. And I hope very much to be with you, although who can tell. We all live in such a dangerous and uncertain world.

(Here I must admit the niggling doubt and fear I had felt not so long ago returned, but I tried to shake off the feeling and moved on)

First, I want you all to agree to have BRITA in charge of operations. None of you would have got to where you are today without her. Neither those of you who already believe in Jesus, nor those of you who still feel you won't or can't.

(I left a little space here so that anyone who wanted to object could do so, but no one did, and I soon continued)

First, I want BRITA to organize a working party to go and really tidy up Hammershus, so that the fortress looks its best, for it is here that I want the main celebrations to take place. And one of the first things you should all consider doing is to gather by the sculpture for prayer, either on your own or in small groups, until you have all been. This will take some time with so many hundreds of people on the island, and this is why we start early.

Second, why not try and get some of the many parts of the fortress working again, as they used to, especially the kitchen. Not forgetting the storerooms and indeed the big meetings halls, where the council used to gather to sentence prisoners. The halls will be good for people to sit and eat and talk and enjoy themselves. Make them look inviting and colourful for everyone. Don't worry about the prison, though, you are so much more peaceful on the island now, there is no need to take any prisoners anymore.

Thirdly, on the highest part of the island, on the spot where I stood not so long ago and tried to finish the sea battle for you, I want you to build and place a wooden cross. It will mark how Jesus died, but most importantly, make sure it is empty, for he did not stay there, and he isn't there now. He is alive, he is forever, and he is here with all of you, as he is with me, sitting here writing this letter.

(Here I stopped for a moment again, for there was a lot to take in, and I was always conscious that not everyone believed what ERLING and I believed. In whom we believed. However, no one raised an eyebrow that I could see, not even among my best friends, so I continued, knowing that we were coming to the end, and that everybody would love the final few paragraphs)

ERLING finished his letter with this:

Those are the main points I want you to work on. It will not be done overnight. It could take weeks. Some of you may not want to take part at first, but I believe most of you will. BRITA will keep you going. Try and bring Hammershus back to its former glory, but this time make it a house of God. Bring in the new! I believe you are ready.

And when the kitchen and the storeroom and the dining halls are finished, BRITA will let MUM take over to do what she does best. You will all eat and drink and be merry, and who knows, perhaps even share little presents, as you do for your own birthdays. I hope to be with you myself, but if not, or if I am late, please, BRITA, keep a note of everything to share with me when I come.

Love to you all. I won't write again, the next time you hear from me will be when I cross the threshold at Hammershus and greet you all with "Hello, Everyone." Just wait and see. With love from ERLING.

(And that was it. The end of the letter. I should have felt elated and happy, and yes, part of me did, but another part felt sad. Would any of us see ERLING again? Then I looked out at the church congregation, and I could not believe what I saw. Everyone, but everyone, were standing and waving their arms around and cheering and shouting, "Praise the Lord, praise Lord Jesus, let's celebrate Christmas, the birth of our Saviour." Well, almost everyone. When all went quiet again, BJORN it was who broke the silence with these words that almost floored me:)

"BRITA, do you not think that once we have rebuilt Hammershus and made everything pretty and warm and lovely, we might come across Thor's hammer after all? I bet it's been lying hidden somewhere all this time and soon, very soon, it will appear."

As we left the church, some were laughing at BJORN's comments – "trust him" – some were shaking their heads – "where *is* he coming from?" – but a few of our people walked up to him, as if they wanted to hear more. Including most of the Icelanders we had treated so well in the infirmary, but who now seemed to still have that Viking blood in them, which made them wonder about that hammer of Thor's.

Once again, I left feeling on a high and at the same time very sad. Knowing that there was a lot to be done in quite a short time, and with a distinct feeling that not everything was right, and that there might well be obstacles in the way. Could I live up to ERLING's expectations of me?

Friday, October 18th

I am sorry it has taken me several days to get back to my Journal, but there was so much to write and remember on the 14th, and I have felt very tired. Anyway, now is the time to get working. I cannot and I must not let ERLING down. Hold on, there's someone at the door. I'll be back soon.

Saturday, October 19th

BJORN it was, come to see me, in tears and obviously distraught. I could but take him in my arms and give him a big cuddle. "What's the matter?"

"It's my fault", he sobbed, "but I couldn't have known. I never meant for this to happen."

"What on earth are you talking about, BJORN," I asked, curious but also mildly irritated at the same time.

"You know when we left church on Sunday and those Icelanders followed me to find out more about Thor's hammer? Well, I told them what I knew, which isn't much, and thought no more of it. But, BRITA, I did tell them where we had been looking for the hammer, and maybe I shouldn't have done that?"

"What's happened, BJORN? What is it you are not telling me?"

"I'm so sorry, BRITA, but they have demolished your sculpture. It's all in ruins now, although I don't think they will ever go back and wreck anything else. Not after the thrashing they got by YULLA and INGRID, not to mention AIFE and RUNE, when they caught up with them. Boy, did they go for them!"

It was then I realized that for the last four days I had kept myself very much to myself, without knowing what had been going on outside. Now I knew. A group of Icelanders had gone in search of the hammer, and some obviously thinking it might be buried by or beneath the sculpture.

"You should have seen it, BRITA," said BJORN, quite excited now, yet still sobbing. "I found a place to hide when I saw the four of them come and run towards the Icelanders. And I tell you, there was no mercy, our friends kicked and threw punches and shouted and hurled stones at the foreigners, and many were hit where it hurt the most. In fact, some could barely walk, when, finally, YULLA said, "Enough!" and brought the battle to an end. But BRITA, the sculpture is demolished, and I cannot see it ever being repaired! And it is all my fault, and I feel so guilty."

I know I should have been angry, and yes, I did feel angry, but more with the Icelanders as with BJORN. How could these strangers treat us like that, after all the care and attention they had received at the infirmary? And being integrated into our community with love and respect. I took BJORN by the hand and said, "Yes, it was a silly thing to do, to tell them where we had been looking for that hammer, but it was even sillier of them to do what they did. Thanks to our friends they got their comeuppance, didn't they, BJORN?" At this he smiled.

"Go on with you, go and find the others. Tell them that tomorrow I will go and inspect the damage, on my own, I don't want anyone else there. Is that clear?"

He nodded and marched off, no doubt feeling very fortunate that he had escaped so easily.

Monday, October 21st

And so, for the first time in ages, if ever, I missed the church service yesterday and went to the sculpture instead. Or the remnants of the sculpture, I should say. BJORN was right, there were not many bits left that one could recognize. Although, after some searching, I did find that Jesus's bronze head and that of Simon Peter were almost undamaged, and to me that meant the world. Jesus, our Lord, and Simon Peter, his favourite disciple, the one he called the Rock, and on whom he built his church. I picked up both bronze heads carefully, and it was then that I just knew what I had to do next.

I remembered ERLING's wish that we erect a wooden cross on the highest point of the island. I decided at this moment that at the foot of that cross the bronze heads of Jesus and Simon Peter would be buried safely in the foundation, on which the cross would stand. Having made this decision, I went home feeling a lot happier than when I set out. I felt quite certain that no one would return here without me knowing about it, so no further damage would be caused.

Wednesday, October 23rd

Today is well and truly the first day of winter. The temperature has dropped overnight, the snow is falling heavily, and I guess it won't be too long before the seas begin to freeze over, as usually happens. So that no one can reach, and no one can leave our island, even if they wanted to.

Regardless of this, work was already starting on the projects ERLING had suggested. The men in the drydock concentrated on the longboats and were busy smartening them up, so they looked brighter than ever before. MUM was busy getting the Hammershus kitchen fit for purpose, and several groups of men worked in rotas on getting the halls ready, where come Christmas we would all be sitting down to eat and be merry. DAD said that this was what he looked forward to most of all.

Seeing that already much was going to plan, I called together my friends and shared with them that I would like just us to go to the highest point and work on that wooden cross. They were all up for it, both those who believed in Jesus, and those who were still not quite sure about or even against him. No one, but no one dared mention Thor and his hammer this time, BJORN least of all.

AIFE and RUNE, the artistic ones, had drawn some sketches of what the cross might look like when in its place, and it looked truly impressive. They were also the ones who immediately started gathering the material needed, followed by the sawing, hammering, binding together with string, and preparing the foundation on a rocky piece of ground. I asked them to leave a couple of small gaps in between the slabs of concrete. When no one looked I went to fetch the two bronze heads and placed them carefully in the gaps, before covering them with bits of grass. Now Jesus and Simon Peter were in place at the foot of the cross, or they would be soon. I felt relieved and moved at the same time and touched my necklace, as I so often did, when I needed comfort and reassurance.

We did not get everything done in one day, but decided to return in a couple of days, when we hoped we could finish the work and fix the cross in place. For everyone on the island to see, and as a watchtower for anyone approaching Bornholm. A sign that this was an island inhabited by Christian people. Well, for the most part anyway.

Saturday, October 26th

The cross is in place, and it looks beautiful. I think because it is empty. It has not got Jesus on it. It could never keep Jesus. He came back to life and is alive here and now. And everywhere. I am sure of it.

We had a short dedication ceremony. I said a few prayers, we sang a psalm or two – just like we do in church – then YULLA and INGRID (being the oldest) said a few words about how fortunate we were to live in such a beautiful place, when we hear so much about the bad and evil going on in other parts of the world. And they also asked us never to forget ERLING and everything he had done for us.

AIFE and RUNE both said how much they liked the finished cross, but of course they had made the sketches, and they had also done much of the hard work. They admitted that they were still unsure about Jesus, but they also agreed that this hammer thing had had its day. If there ever were such a thing, it ought to remain buried.

FRIDA and LEIF did not have a lot to say, but they were good at keeping an eye on LOVA and BJORN, which was good. And finally, little SKOL was happy in his own little world, still not crawling, but smiling happily at everyone he came across. Always happy he was.

As for me, BRITA, I am just so pleased that such good work has been done, and I reckon the cross stands tall enough on its hilltop to be seen from a very long distance. It will be the first thing ERLING notices when he returns to Bornholm. And then it hits me again, *will* he in fact be returning? I still have this niggling doubt and feeling that not all is well, although of course he has only been gone for a month. And America is a long way from here, a new world completely for us.

Tuesday, October 29th

It is incredible, but we have only been working on all the things that ERLING suggested in his letter for just over a week, and already most of it is in place. This is because everybody on the island gave a hand, including the Icelanders, and even some of those who had been guilty of smashing the sculpture. They obviously did not want to be at the sharp end of AIFE and RUNE's fists again and had the decency to find them and talk to them after a few days. They also promised never to do anything like this again. You could almost say they apologized, though not in so many words.

THE PRIESTS, seeing how quickly all the work had proceeded, made the decision to have a service of thanksgiving and dedication on Sunday. They had the courtesy to come and see me about it, as after all I am the Princess. I almost jumped in to say that of course we had already had our own little service at the foot of the cross, but I bit my tongue. How terrible would it be if our cross got a second mention and blessing in their service? Why shouldn't it?

I told all my friends what was going to happen on Sunday morning, and they promised to turn up. Even those among us who did not yet believe, and perhaps never would.

Friday, November 1st

DAD came to see me today, and I did not like the look on his face! My first thought was that I must have done something wrong or something to upset him, and it was only when he took my hand and asked me to sit down with him that I relaxed a bit.

"BRITA," he started, "I don't know about you, but I am worried about the reports we keep hearing that there is a lot of war and strife going on around us. And I am especially concerned about the rumours that some Vikings, a long way from here, are determined to put their lives at risk in England and on the French coast, maybe not right now, but in years to come. Why cannot people learn to live in peace with one another?"

I looked at him for a little while and could not help smiling, as I said, "Well, DAD, to be honest, it is not that long ago that you, yes you, would have been among the first to go into battle, without thinking too long about it. Or have you forgotten your expedition to Norway, where of course you first met ERLING? You did not exactly go there with good cheer and best wishes for the Norwegians, did you, DAD?"

He looked at me pensively for a moment and then, with a twinkle in his eye, said, "Yes, ERLING. I wonder how he is getting on. Do you think he will make it back to us in time for Christmas? He said he would like to."

"I don't know, DAD. It is a long way to America, and for all we know he is not even there yet. And we cannot know what reception he will have once he arrives. Both ERLING, and of course your oarsmen as well, we must not forget them."

DAD left a few moments after this, and I don't think he even realized that he had not replied to my comments about his temper and love for going to war not that very long ago. And yet, I was not going to remind him. I liked DAD the way he was now, and so did everybody on the island. I may be the Princess, but DAD is our leader, the chieftain, the commander, and we all know and respect that.

Sunday, November 3rd

It was a lovely service this morning, and every single room and tower in the island that had been rebuilt was remembered by name and prayed for and blessed. We all left the two churches feeling that soon we could start really preparing for Christmas. We would let MUM take control of that side of things, as of course much of it would have something to do with food!

The weather is already wintry, and some would say dismal and dark. The days are getting shorter and shorter, and there is a limit to what can be done outdoors now. The cattle are kept in their comfortable stables and barns and being well looked after. The ships in the shipyard have been covered up for the winter, as by now the seas have frozen, and no one can enter or leave. Who would want to leave Bornholm anyway? The best place to be in the whole world for sure.

Not that YULLA and INGRID think so! They are still feeling sorry for themselves that ERLING did not respond the way they had hoped. What could be better than have a tall, handsome giant of a Norwegian warrior to cuddle up to and keep you warm? But alas, it was not to be, and now there was nowhere else for them to go and look, not for a few months, at least.

The rest of us have no problem finding things to do inside, and for me there is no warmer feeling that to sit by the fire and write my Journal, or pray, or read again the wonderful letters I have received through the year. The one written by THE PRIEST, and of course ERLING's two, which I treasure most of all.

I do wonder just sometimes whether I too have a soft spot for ERLING? If so, I 'd better not tell YULLA and INGRID. And in any case, I am far too young for him.

Wednesday, November 6th

You could have blown me over with a feather when yesterday I received yet another message from ERLING. I really had not expected to hear from him again, and he had said so himself, and still, here he was, in contact with me, once more.

This time it was to say that he and DAD's men have finally arrived in America and that they enjoy a friendly welcome by the natives there. He also writes that there is plenty of opportunity to talk about Jesus. Although, to be honest, the natives seem to worship so many other gods – not just the likes of Odin and Thor (whom in fact they had never even heard of) – that it is likely to be an uphill battle to get them converted. If ever…

However, ERLING writes that he is happy to stay on for a while, until the middle of the month perhaps. Which might just give him enough time to get back to us in time for Christmas, and assuming of course that the seas have defrosted by then.

It was when I got to the last paragraph that my heart almost stopped for a moment and I had trouble reading on, as the tears began to flow, and I could not control them.

"BRITA, whatever happens, and you can never tell, know this: I have never known anyone so loving and kind and faithful as you. Not ever. I know DAD always calls you his Princess, and I can see why. You have a heart of gold, you can listen and act in a good spirit, and you are willing to take time with those of your friends who are not yet sure about Jesus. You are happy to answer questions. I admire you and yes, I love you. There you have it: I love you. Perhaps not in the sense that YULLA and INGRID are always dreaming about, but in a different and much better sense, the spiritual one. I really do believe you and I are of one spirit, BRITA, and being away from you has only served to confirm my belief. So, this comes with all my love. If I make just a little headway here in America, it is because I know you are praying for me to succeed. I can ask for no more. God bless you, BRITA.

Yours

ERLING"

Friday, November 8th

I spent much of yesterday quietly thinking about ERLING's message, and this made me consider, not for the first time, why it was that even some of my best friends found it so hard to believe in God and Jesus.

I think I have mentioned this before, or perhaps heard someone else mention it, that one reason may be that Jesus just sounds too good to be true. Simple as that. Perhaps more people than we think really *want* to believe in him, but just cannot take it all in and make him real to them. But then I ask myself, why is it that I have never really doubted him, once I got to know about him, and don't find him too difficult at all? The PRIESTS have suggested to me that it may have to do with my faith, which is a very personal thing, and that perhaps my faith is greater than others.

This sounds a bit big-headed to me, and I hope it isn't true, because if faith is a personal thing, then there does not seem to be much one can do change somebody's mind. I would love YULLA and INGRID and AIFE and RUNE to come round to my way of thinking first, and then maybe the others after that, but I don't know if I shall ever manage it.

I know what ERLING would say, if he had been here: "Keep at it, girl, don't give up. What **you** have needs to be shared with others, for it is the best news there is: that Jesus came to live with us, die for us, and be risen again to life for us."

Simple, when you think about it like that, only it isn't. It is a lot to take in.

Friday, November 15th

A whole week gone and no journal notes! It really isn't good enough, BRITA. Shame on you! No, seriously, one reason why I have been absent for a while is that following a couple of outings with my friends to the cross, I feel I am getting to know them better than ever, and to understand a little more where they are coming from. That does not mean that I always agree with everything they think or say, far from it, but I am realizing that everyone is entitled to their own opinions, and that we do not always have to agree on everything to remain friends.

These are some of the comments I have had directed at me during the week. I shared some of them with the two PRIESTS, and interestingly, neither of them said, "Don't believe a word of it, BRITA, you just stick to your guns." No, they smiled sweetly and nodded, almost as if they had heard it all before. And perhaps they had?

This is some of what I heard from my friends, and so as not to embarrass anyone, I don't give any names.

"I have to admit that this Jesus has made our island a lot more peaceful, and quiet too, and people seem to have more time and respect for one another."

"Is it true that being a Christian means we are worshipping the only God who ever came down to this earth to find us, rather than a god who will always expect us to look upwards to heaven and find him?"

"It is all very well, but I do miss the old battles we used to have, and play as kids, all that seems to have gone now, so much of the fun has gone."

"Why is it that Jesus never seems to be near to me when I want or need him the most? I can think of many times recently when I really felt down and could have done with his presence. But no, I certainly did not feel him anywhere close. Perhaps he was busy caring for someone else?"

"It is not that I do not want to believe, I do, but often when I try, I seem to get diverted. Something, or someone, inside me, tries to get me to go the other way, the old way, and sometimes I agree that the old way seemed so much more fun."

"I wonder if ERLING ever asks the same questions that we now do, or whether he has the love and patience to listen to other opinions than his own? How is he getting on in that foreign land with all those natives, I ask myself? OK, so we have Odin and Thor, or we did, I am not so sure now. While over there they seem to have countless more gods than that. Or do they just make them up as they go along?"

"If Jesus came in peace and love, and if the world a thousand years ago was just as full of hate and war and strife as it is now, how come he did not change all that there and then? Why do we still have to suffer so much, maybe not us, but many in the world that we hear about?"

"Do we have a choice whether to believe in God and Jesus or not? And are we doomed if we decide not to? Is there hope for those who find it difficult, yet keep searching? Can anyone really love everyone, even if not everyone loves Him?"

"Will there ever be peace, real peace, here on earth? Will Jesus really come back one day and put everything right?"

And finally, this one:

"I am so glad I am no longer bothered about Thor's hammer! The Cross that BRITA built is so much grander and more significant, overlooking so much of our beautiful coast and stormy seas. It makes me feel safe. I cannot understand it, but this Cross makes me feel warm inside."

Can you now see why it has taken me a while to get back to the journal? Lots to ponder. And I know I said I would not mention any names, and I haven't, except I guess you all know who brought up the matter of the hammer again? Except, he too seems to have changed his tune.

Meanwhile, preparations for Christmas are continuing well. I do not see much of MUM and DAD. They are far too busy organizing and putting things in place for the big event. I wonder if ERLING will make it back in time. I do hope so, but the seas are still frozen and passage in or out impossible.

Sunday, November 17th

Although we have still over a month to go to Christmas, the two PRIESTS took time in their services this morning to read and share about the birth of Jesus. How he came as a Babe, was born in a stable, and even thinking about what the animals surrounding him must have felt? Not to mention the shepherds, who were the first to hear the good news, poor and lonely as they were.

The PRIESTS explained that shepherds at the time of Jesus' birth were outcasts and not counted for much by anyone. And yet, God chose **them** to be the first to hear that the Saviour was born. The farmers among us, and there are many, felt truly blessed by this information, I could tell, and many told the PRIESTS at the end of the services how much their words had meant to them.

Tuesday, November 19th

For the first time ever the PRIEST from Malta decided to join our little group at the Cross this morning. No one had invited him. My friends and I were getting so used to this being our own little private meeting, but nor did we mind having him with us. On the contrary. We sensed immediately that he had something on his heart he needed to share with us.

I invited him to start us off with a prayer, and he did so. A short time of quiet reflection followed, and then the PRIEST began.

"My dear friends," he started, "you may wonder what I am doing here. And I will tell you. Like you, I am waiting eagerly for ERLING to return, and I do believe the weather may be about to change slightly and the seas begin to thaw. I hope so. You see, ERLING has for a long time reminded me of PAUL, the apostle and follower of Jesus. Who travelled wide and far, who shipwrecked in Malta, as I think you already have heard about, and managed almost single-handedly to convert the whole Maltese population to Jesus."

I nodded, for yes, I had heard this mentioned before by that other PRIEST from Malta, who sadly died, and I wondered what would be coming now. Most of my friends looked puzzled or quite uninterested, so I thought this had better be good.

And the PRIEST did not disappoint.

"When I first came across ERLING, I thought well, here is another tall and handsome, blond Norwegian Viking, just like so many of the others I have come across over the years. But how wrong I was. ERLING is someone very special, and just like PAUL, he is not afraid to travel the world and spread the good news. However, I want to share with you today that not all of us are called or expected to do the same. Many of us are simply asked to do good and speak well of Jesus right here where we are. And I tell you now, it makes a great difference when we do."

"Look at BRITA," he said (and I did not know where to put myself), "she is a shining example to all of you, to all of us. To me. And to ERLING. And ERLING knew this when he decided to travel to the other side of the world. And he knew that he could safely leave BRITA in charge here, however young she may be. Why? You may ask. And how? Well, I will tell you now."

"BRITA it was who never complained, never got angry, never sought revenge even when her beloved sculpture was smashed. BRITA it was who found and salvaged the bronze heads of Jesus and Simon Peter and made them part of the foundation of this Cross, on which it stands. And BRITA it was who enabled the Cross to be erected in the first place and stand where it now is, overlooking the island, but also the first sign of Jesus anyone will see when they arrive at our island, and from wherever they come."

I really wished the PRIEST would stop. I was feeling quite embarrassed, but he had more on his heart.

"Whatever you believe, or not, however difficult you find it to become a Christian, never give up, but speak to BRITA, listen to her, learn from her, argue with her if you wish. For she will take time to listen and teach and never get angry or disappointed with you. She will take the time you need, each one of you. No one comes to Jesus in the same way or at the same time, and BRITA knows that. As does ERLING. They are two of a kind."

With that the PRIEST took my hand and held it to his heart, as with my other hand I took hold of the empty cross, my necklace, and held it tighter and for longer than ever before. And I remained standing there and holding on to it long after the PRIEST and my friends had quietly left for home.

Friday, November 22nd

Time goes so fast that it is a job to keep up with it all. And reports keep coming in about Viking battles taking place in so many parts of the world, most of which I have not even heard about before. It looks like our people, the Vikings (and I can tend to forget sometimes that of course I **am** one myself) are intent on conquering the world. So why is it we keep losing, and our numbers keep falling? That is worrying. DAD told me only the other day that there may be less than 10,000 of us left in the whole world, and he also said that some of our greatest warriors are abiding time, and quietly planning for the conquest of Britain and Normandy. They know this will be their greatest, perhaps final, battle ever, and they also know that they cannot rush into it. DAD says this will take years, perhaps even decades, before it can happen.

"Do you wish you could be part of that battle, DAD?", I asked. He thought for a moment, then took my hand and said quietly, "No worries there, my little Princess. I will be long dead and gone before it happens, mark my words."

Now, I know for a fact that at the beginning of this year, and had I asked him the same question, he would have donned his full armour, called his men together and rushed to the docks to board his ships, before I had even finished the sentence! So much has changed here in such a short time that I can barely take it in.

Sunday, November 24th

Precisely a month now to Holy Night (as the PRIESTS insist on calling Christmas), and already the preparations are practically finished. I have never seen so much food prepared and safely stored at Hammershus, and DAD will be pleased to know that there is no shortage of beer and wine either. However, for me the best thing of all is that the PRIESTS loved my suggestion when I said to them that I would like – with the help of my friends of course – to build a crib, just like the one Jesus was placed in. Then place it by the Cross for everyone to go and see. They both thought it was a marvellous idea and added that perhaps we could create a donkey as well, and some figurines of Mary and Joseph and the shepherds to complete the picture? And why not place an angel and a star at the top of the Cross, just to finish everything off nicely?

I was not sure whether the PRIESTS were being just a little sarcastic, but as I am always up for a challenge, I said yes, knowing that I have some very creative friends who will just love to get stuck in with this. What a Christmas – or Holy Night – this is already panning out to be. I cannot wait.

Monday, November 25th

And today, finally, the seas began to defrost, it looks like the big freeze may be over (although you can never be sure, it may well return later). Winters are like that here, you think you know where you have them, but you don't, and they can come back with a vengeance at any moment. But for now, all is good, and ERLING, there is no excuse for you not to say goodbye to America and head home to us! I reckon if you set sails now, you'll just about make it. We all miss you so much.

Wednesday, November 27th

Today news arrived that the relatively few Vikings they have in Finland – hundreds rather than thousands – have come under threat from neighbouring Russia. Or the Big Bear as Finland often calls their neighbour. Thankfully it also appears that the Vikings are being well supported and backed up by those Fins who do not count themselves as Vikings, and as they number tens of thousands and are well equipped and battle ready, the Big Bear had better watch out! But this is just another sign that things are not good in the big wide world, and no one can count themselves completely safe. Not ever. And when you think about it, neither Finland nor Russia are all that far removed from us.

The PRIESTS reminded us yet again on Sunday that it was always like this. The Holy Land was occupied by the Romans when Jesus was born, and war and strife never really ceased. But they also assured us that it is NOT that God wants wars and strife to happen, and it is NOT that he could not put a stop to them all, should he so desire. The fact is, they say, that the biggest gift God ever gave people like us, people everywhere, good and bad, is the gift of Free Will. Most people choose to do good, but some there are who will always choose to cause chaos. If God suddenly decided that he had to step in and sort us all out for good and for once, then he would have to take away from us the greatest gift he ever gave us in the first place. He cannot, he will not do that. He will rather wait for as long as it takes for us to come to our senses.

I must admit that when the PRIESTS really get going like this, I find them quite hard to follow. And if I find them hard to understand, no wonder some of my friends have already given up! Somehow, Odin and Thor seem a much safer and easier option. Only, they are nowhere near as real as Jesus can be to us, if only we let him into our hearts and minds.

Saturday, November 30th

I just knew it! I have felt it in my heart for some time but did not want to share it with anyone else, not even the PRIESTS. And certainly not with my friends, for I knew what many of them would say. "We told you so. Your God, your Jesus cannot be trusted. Just see what he is allowing to happen now …"

Reports are coming in that yes, indeed, ERLING has left America, apparently fit and well as are all DAD's men on the ship he lent them. That's something at least. However, instead of heading back to Bornholm, they are now on their way to Finland! And knowing ERLING, they are going there to tackle the Big Bear, Russia. Good luck to them, that's all I can say. A couple of dozen men against one of the biggest nations in the world. This cannot end well, and I fear that no amount of Jesus talk by ERLING will make any difference to the outcome.

It will be Christmas without ERLING. In fact, I doubt if any of us will ever see him alive again? Why couldn't he just accept that this is one battle too many, even for him?

As I am thinking these things, it is then it comes to me that in fact there is a lesson to be learnt even now. And I remember ERLING's parting words to me and his belief that Bornholm is safe with me in charge. I wish I could share his optimism right now. Frankly, I am frightened.

My friends are so busy building the figurines of Mary and Joseph, Baby Jesus in the crib, the donkey and the shepherds, the Bethlehem Star, and the angel that I haven't got the heart to tell them the news. Mind you, they may have heard anyway, but if so, they are not letting on. Nor are the PRIESTS for that matter. Perhaps they are thinking if only we carry on regardless, all will be well?

So, what is the lesson I am learning? It is not easy to explain, but I think it has to do with the fact that it is only by inviting Jesus into your heart and mind that you begin to realize that you do not need the actual person, someone to see and touch. Jesus within you is all it takes for that feeling of calm, security, and love, against all the odds. To have the courage to believe, and the faith to keep your belief alive.

All I can do now is pray for ERLING and DAD'S men, and I do. But the words do not seem to come, and most of what I pray are no more than quiet thoughts from within, where words do not exist, and perhaps are not required?

Monday, December 2nd

Things seem to happen very quickly now in the big, wide world. It appears that Norway and indeed neutral Sweden (Sweden never enters any conflict if they can avoid it) are joining forces with Finland in facing up to Russia. How that is going to work out, only God knows. Seriously. And whether this will change anything ERLING has in mind, or whether he will even know, remains to be seen. I am not holding my breath either way.

DAD can tell that something is playing on my mind, and MUM as well. I can see they really want to come and hold me and talk to me, and I need both for sure, but there is too much I cannot make sense of, and I cannot explain to them.

Instead, I try to fill my days with meeting up with my friends to do all that important work by the Cross, and it is coming on nicely. Every now and again we look across the ocean to see if there might just be a ship or two approaching, although as things look, if there were, they would probably be heading much further north, towards Finland. There is nothing to see at present. It is as if Bornholm is left to its own devices, which is not surprising really, as we are but a pleasant little bit of rock in the mighty sea.

Thursday, December 5th

The Bear has retreated – for now. Hearing that substantial forces were on their way to assist Finland, it seems that the mighty empire has decided to withdraw, if only for a while. Until another opportunity arises, no doubt. That seems to be the way of the world.

Some of the ships that were heading for Finland are now doing a slight detour and are coming our way. My heart beats with excitement, for these will be the first visitors to see our Cross and the nativity scene that is now complete. And they will know that they are coming to a Christian country, where peace reigns and God is in control. We can count about three or four ships so far, and if we assume about twenty people on each longboat, our numbers could soon swell by almost a hundred people. We told MUM so that she could start preparing some extra food, assuming the visitors will stay with us over Christmas. DAD is worried about his supplies of beer! Will there be enough?

Strangely, no one on the island seem in the least bit concerned as to whether we are about to welcome friends or enemies. Not so long ago we would have manned Hammershus, checked that the cannons were ready for action, and prepared the longboats for battle, just in case, but not now. We just waited.

Saturday, December 7th

So, here we are, with another complement of visitors among us. Almost a hundred of them, from Norway and Sweden and even a few Greenlanders and Icelanders among them too. I think just as well the Big Bear had second thoughts, or he might well have been in for a nasty surprise!

So many new languages and dialects to get used to, and yet, in a funny kind of way, we all seem to understand one another. Some are obviously Vikings, and proud of it, while others look and act nothing like Vikings at all. Most surprising of all, however, is the fact that there are small children and teenagers among them, which of course is great for my friends and me, as we get to know one another. But I do wonder what use the young ones would have been in battle, had it come to that?

The PRIESTS have encouraged everyone on the island to warmly welcome these strangers and invite them to stay for as long as they like. And once they saw MUM's kitchen and DAD's beer and wine cellars at Hammershus, not one hesitated in anchoring their boats in our docks and covering them up for the winter. Obviously in no rush to leave in a hurry, if ever! Praise the Lord.

I cannot know, but I just have this feeling that what is happening now is important. To all of us. The fact that we Vikings are being visited by many who are not. The whole feeling that change is about to happen, and that from now on we are all simply going to be **people,** real **people,** with no labels, but together in respect and love for one another. ERLING would be pleased!

And as I prepare for sleep, I come to see how in time, and with so many different ages and backgrounds on the island, people from different traditions will marry. And children will be born who couldn't care less whether they are Vikings or not but can rejoice in having found a new land, where Jesus is at the centre.

For the first time in I don't know how many days, I can go to sleep with a real lightness of heart and peace of mind.

Monday, December 9th

The church services, yesterday, were so special and beautiful, and some people seemed to not only stand but almost hang from the rafters, to see and hear. Never have our churches been so packed! The PRIESTS offered the sermons, but they also asked DAD to speak words of welcome as the chieftain, the head of the island, and he did so with lots of enthusiasm. Alright, I guess the PRIESTS thought he talked about food and beer a bit too much, but they let him get on with it, and the visitors certainly did not seem to mind.

This was not my time to speak as the Little Princess of the island, but I knew my day would come soon enough. My friends and I, including many of the children from among the visitors, went to the Cross after lunch, where we just sat and prayed and admired the figurines for a very long time, before returning home. I did cast a glance out over the sea, just in case… But no, there was no other boat in sight, not for as far as my eyes could see anyway.

Tuesday, December 10th

Just two weeks to go to Holy Night, and all is in place. Decorations are up, tables are laid, beer barrels filled. There simply isn't anything left to do, except be patient and continue to quietly prepare. For the coming of Jesus, as we shall party and remember how he came to this earth almost a thousand years ago. And, if we believe the PRIESTS, look forward to his coming again one day.

Of course, it is still winter, but it is a mild one, and the seas have not frozen up again. I just hope and pray that they will stay like this for as long as possible. Not that I want anyone to leave, but who knows who might still arrive and come to live among us?

Most of all, I pray for peace throughout the world, but I know that this is not likely to happen quickly. DAD will often remind me that it is often at the most important seasons of the Christian year, like Christmas, that the worst accidents seem to happen. I do wonder why that is…

Thursday, December 12th

I mentioned only the other day that the Russian Bear has had second thoughts about invading Finland. Reports are now coming in that it might not just have been the support Finland received from Greenland, Norway, Sweden, and other nations that made him think twice. New-found America too has joined in the fun and has assured us here in the West that we need never feel forgotten or alone, should something similar happen again. What great news this is, although of course America is a very long way from here. It will take the natives time to assemble their armies and journey across.

I wonder if their promise has anything to do with ERLING's visit. I guess I shall never know, but it is a nice thought.

One other thing that has happened rather quickly is the way that YULLA and INGRID have integrated with the many different nations, who arrived here so recently. In fact, rumour has it that the girls have finally found some attractive young men, with whom they seem to spend a lot of time. And I **have** noticed that they do not seem to have time to join the rest of us as often by the Cross as they used to. Never mind. AIFE and RUNE (bless them, they did most of the work on the figurines by far) FRIDA and LEIF, and even LOVA, BJORN and SKOLL seem happy to continue to keep me company. "BRITA," they will often say, "isn't it time we went and sat by the Cross again for a little while?", and my heart beats with love and gratitude whenever I hear those words. Little SKOLL has stopped crawling now and is beginning to find his feet. This is where we shall all need eyes in the back of our heads to keep track of him, I'm sure.

It is funny, whenever I write down all their names and compare where they are now to how they started almost a year ago, I realize how much has changed. How much **they** have changed. Perhaps YULLA and INGRID most of all, who seem to be making a new start with people. Most of whom no longer see themselves as Vikings, but all of whom see themselves as Christian people living on this island of Bornholm.

Sunday, December 15th

As you would expect, getting this close to Christmas, the church services this morning were exceptionally well attended, with lots of praying, singing, meditation and of course wise words from the PRIESTS in their sermons. All the decorations and lights everywhere added to the whole atmosphere of expectation and warmth and security. Yes, security, for although we were aware of all the bad things happening in the world, Christmas brought home to us promises of even better days to come. And indeed, of a time when all earthly strife would cease completely and Jesus, our God, be known and worshipped everywhere. I truly believe this, and I am glad to see and hear that at least half the island's population feel the same. Yes, there are some who cannot or will not let go off the old ways, of how things used to be, and I guess it will always be like that, but more and more are coming to Jesus for hope and joyfulness.

Tuesday, December 17th

My friends and I decided yesterday that getting so close to Christmas now, this would be our last joint gathering at the Cross. I suggested that from now on and until Holy Night, those of us who wanted to go alone and find a quiet place here could and should do so. And those who didn't, or might not feel they needed to, could stay at home, and no one would think any worse of them for that. As I reminded them, Jesus it is who gave us all the gift of Free Will, to enable us to make up our own minds. Yet always assuring us that wherever we found ourselves, he would be right there with us. In our doubts, our questioning, our searching.

They all seemed happy with that, and after a time of prayer, we went our own ways quietly. I admit that from now on I did not expect to see many of them again until Christmas. And in a strange kind of way, I **hoped** I wouldn't, as I felt I still had a lot of private reflection to do on my own, by the Cross, the Crib, and all the figurines making up the Christmas scene, as it must have looked on that first Holy Night.

Tuesday, December 24th Christmas Eve/Holy Night

And so, we are there! Together with Easter the most important date in the Christian calendar, when we celebrate the birth of our Lord, Jesus Christ. I am dotting this down, sitting by the Cross, after a very full day of festivities, carol singing, praying, listening to sermons, and, of course, eating and drinking to excess. DAD and his men especially, I don't think we shall see or hear much from them tomorrow!

YULLA and INGRID are spending Christmas with their newfound friends, and good for them, and most of my other nephews and nieces are spending time with their families, doing whatever they feel like doing, and many of them playing with their new toys. Christmas is a time for giving, just like God gave Jesus to us, and Jesus, finally, gave himself for each one of us.

I have been taking part in most of the celebrations today, but now, as evening sets in, I find myself by the Cross once again, looking out over the sea, still and calm it is, as if the waves also recognize the importance of this season. I look across as far as my eyes can see, and at first, I see nothing unusual. As my eyes get more accustomed to the dark, I do finally detect something on the very far horizon, too distant yet to tell what it is. But could it be, might it just be? Him! A bit late for Holy Night, but in good time for the New Year? Realizing that nothing will be revealed tonight, I decide to go home but return tomorrow night. My heart is beating faster than it has been for days, as I grip my necklace and hold on to it for dear life, slowly leaving the Cross behind.

Thursday, December 26th

Yes, it is him! ERLING is on his way back to us. And DAD's oarsmen of course. I recognize the colours and symbols of the sails as the longboat slowly but surely gets closer. It will be another day or two before they get here by my reckoning, but I will return to the Cross, as I did last night, for as long as it takes, and I will not tell anyone. My ERLING is returning home! And as I say those words to myself, I realize that this is the first time I have referred to him as **my** ERLING. What is happening to me? How **dare** I presume…? And yet, I sense a deep feeling of peace and reassurance as once more I head for home, determined to be back until he steps onto that beach and holds me in his arms.

Sunday, December 29th

Never have I spent this much time getting ready for Sunday service! But then again, never have I had so much to look forward to. I know for a fact that I shall not be able to concentrate on anything at all the PRIESTS may have to say this morning. I shall be far too busy looking admiringly at the handsome, tall young man, ERLING, who will be sitting next to me, keeping me company. He has promised!

Alright, you can tell he hasn't shaved for a very long while, and yes, he could do with a good, long bath, but now that he has had a day or two to get used to being home again, all the rest will follow. I will make sure of it for him. My ERLING! Who can believe it?

I know there can never be anything romantic happening between us, the age gap is just too big. But I know also that he will always be here with me and for me from now on, for there is a deep and real Christian love and understanding between us. I really do believe he has finished with his travels now. Knowing ERLING, wherever he has been on his return journey, he will have taught others how to carry on the good work. And I know now that the reason why he did not make it home for Christmas was the fact that he stopped briefly in several foreign ports, as he had important work to do. "Just like PAUL," he told me. "I wanted to try and be just like PAUL, if only for a while."

And so, we come to the end of the Journal. The church bells are calling us to service. I can see ERLING coming up the path towards me, just as he promised he would. To keep me company, not just at church this morning, but every day for the rest of our lives, and beyond. Whatever the future may hold. I am sure of it.

My ERLING. My Jesus. My God. Right here and right now.

THE END

The Viking longboat in a Norwegian Fiord

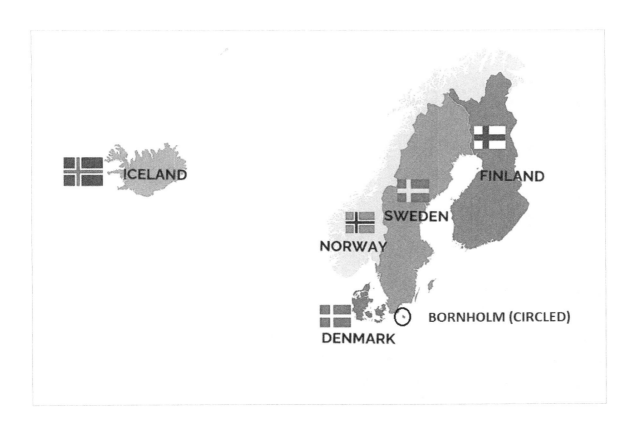

SUPPLEMENT 1

Selected drawings by Esme Harvey (or might we call her BRITA?), the little PRINCESS, 9 years of age (November 2023).

Brita aka the Viking Princess with Hammershus in the background

Hammershus on The Island of Bornholm Standing tall to this day

A Typical Viking Settlement Layout

A Viking homestead Scene

Family – Orientated
Loving
Caring
Peaceful

Another Happy Viking family. Vikings were mostly hard-working farmers and ship-builders, famous for their spectacular longboats.

A Viking pagan temple where they worshipped Odin and Thor

A typical example of an early Viking church and graveyard

Erling – One of the most impressive and important characters in the book (Although you have to wait for him to appear !)

JUST A FEW FACTS AND FIGURES ABOUT THE VIKING ERA

Very few Vikings were as violent and quarrelsome as history wants us to believe they were. Most of them were farmers and seagoing folk, always interested in exploring new horizons, but mostly well behaved and easy enough to get on with.

The Viking used the Rune alphabet to communicate. It did not have nearly as many letters as ours today. In my book, BRITA receives a lot of 'letters', although of course 'letters' as we know them today did not exist in the year 1000, nor did the Post Office! Often people would 'write' by using a hammer and chisel to inscribe their messages on rock or stone, and then, whoever found them (wherever in the world they might be), and read them, would pass them on, either by finding other rocks or big stones to write the messages on, OR by way of smoke signals to forward the messages. So, it was a VERY different way of communication to ours. However, for the purposes of my book, we do not worry too much about how and in what format BRITA gets her messages, but more about what they contain.

Christianity did come to Denmark and the other Scandinavian countries around 1000 AD, which is when our story takes place. And Jesus and his message did eventually cancel out the pagan worship of Odin and Thor, for which the Vikings are renowned. In time, their pagan temples were replaced by Christian churches.

CHRISTIANIA was indeed the original name of the Norwegian capital city, and it was built from scratch round about the year 1000 AD. It was many centuries later that CHRISTIANIA was renamed OSLO (as we know it today). Also, GUDHJEM – God's Abode – is the capital city of the island of Bornholm. GODTHAAB – the port of GOOD HOPE – is the capital city of Greenland.

By the year 1000 AD, Christianity had gained foothold in many parts of the world, including the Scandinavian countries, and pagan worship of Odin and Thor was dwindling. By the time of our story, CHRISTMAS, the birth of Christ, was already well established and in the book properly celebrated. EASTER too was a high season always remembered by many, although for the purposes of this book only briefly referred to, as my action begins in early 1000AD while tensions between paganism and Christianity were still ripe and unsolved and the true message of Easter not yet ready to be shared.

In 1066, the Vikings arrived at Normandy and England, and this became the beginning of the end for the Vikings as we like to remember them – warriors and plunderers, nasty people all round. Only, as mentioned above, for most it wasn't necessarily so.

And finally, this: Soon after 1000 AD, the Norwegian explorer LEIF ERIKSEN and his crew reached America, 400 years before Christopher Columbus in fact! LEIF did not come to fight, he came in peace, and he came to proclaim Jesus to another new nation. My character ERLING is loosely based on LEIF ERIKSEN.

And in case you wondered about the meaning of the name ERLING. Well, it translates "Descendant of the Lord of the Manor", and for many of us alive in the world today, Jesus is our "Lord of the Manor", and we are indeed his followers, His "descendants."

Thanks be to God.

Preben Andersen

The Reverend Preben Andersen is a Methodist minister of religion, who, at the age of 73, has now enjoyed his first three years of retirement from active ministry, to concentrate on his life-long ambition of writing books. He is of Danish origin but domiciled in Britain since 1977. His writing has proven to appeal to Christians and non-Christians alike, and he has written numerous regular articles to the secular press over the years. His aim is always to point people to Christ, but in a non-threatening, gentle and often humorous way.

Preben now has five books with Amazon Kindle in paperback and e-reader formats, i.e. "Living Through Lockdown", "Thought for the Weak", "A Collection of Short Stories", "It Shouldn't Happen to a Reverend", and now his latest offering, "A Year in the Life of a Viking Princess".

Next in line is "Dorothy's Treasure", which is his project for 2024. He aims to write one new book a year, for as long as God gives him the power to do so, and all his works are and will continue to be stand-alone, rather than one, particular series of books. He feels this gives him the best scope to try out a multitude of subjects and strands, whereas series of books can tend to limit such exploration.

Printed in Great Britain
by Amazon

39858817R00053